A PARANORMAL HORROR

TRAGEDY

MEGAN KIRRMANN

Design and distribution by Bublish

ISBN: 979-8-89989-090-1 (Paperback)

Contents

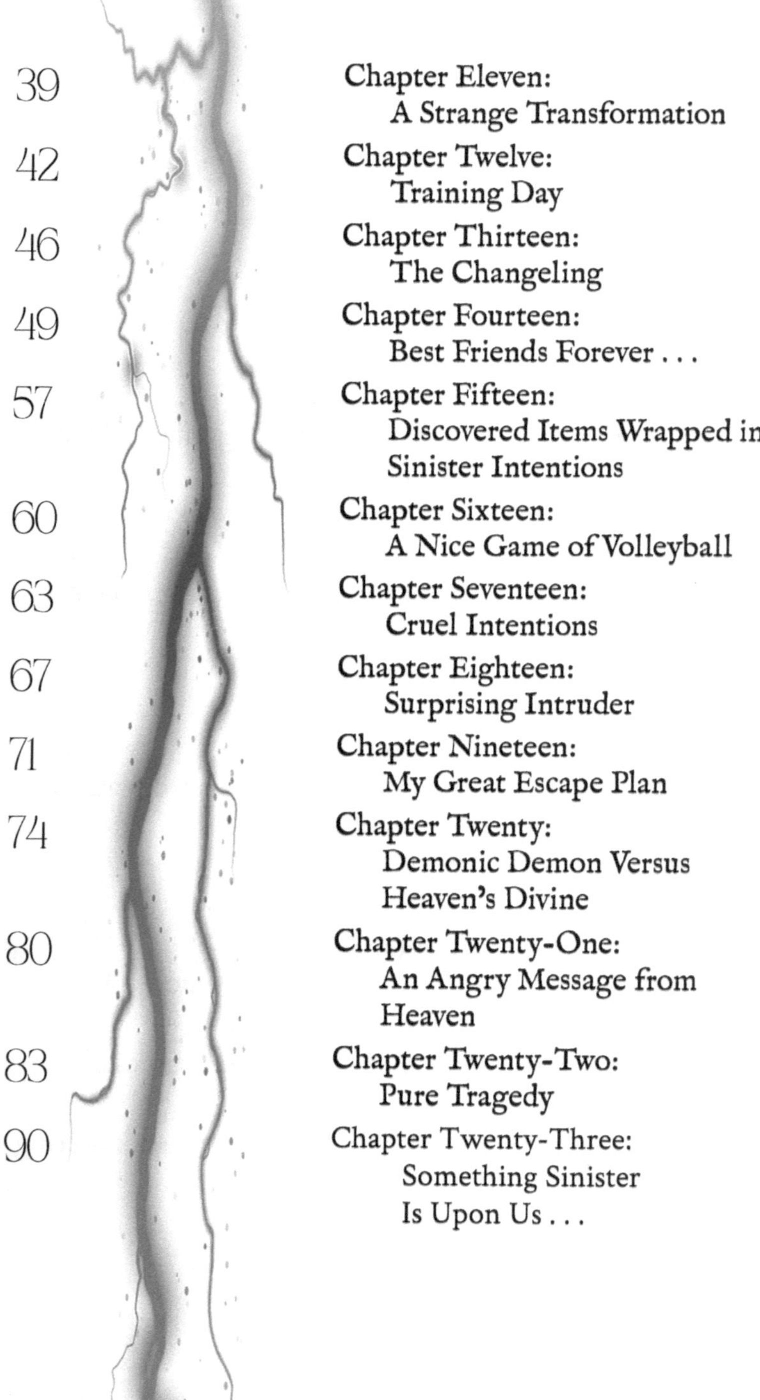

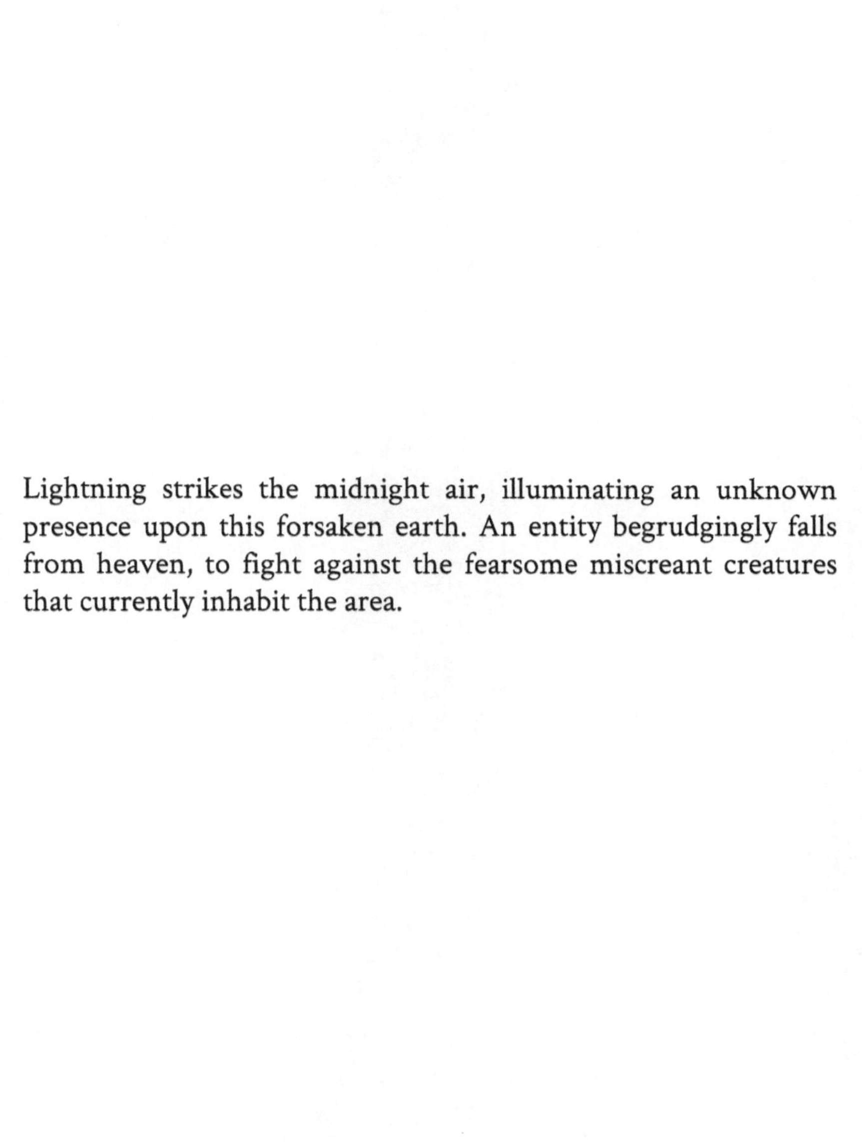

Lightning strikes the midnight air, illuminating an unknown presence upon this forsaken earth. An entity begrudgingly falls from heaven, to fight against the fearsome miscreant creatures that currently inhabit the area.

Chapter One

AFTERNOON OF AGONIZING PAIN

Later the next day, at 3:00 p.m. in the afternoon.

Racing footsteps pounded the ice-cold pavement. The sounds that echoed behind me were the only distinctive noises.

"On time . . . everything has to be in order . . . my order . . . I will soon announce the time," whispered in my ear. The menacing shadow at my back kept pace. I was trying to run away from my abusive ex-boyfriend, but I was solely focused on finding some type of safe house, or anything really, to finally escape him. Was it all a lie? Everything we went through together? A glance over my feminine shoulder adorned with a butterfly tattoo witnessed empty concrete pavement.

Quickly, I made my way toward the cathedral, with its ebony spires, which gave the building an overall intimidating appearance. Several seconds later, I realized I could not physically allow myself to enter the cathedral. I tried to take my hand off the door handle, but it would not move. A searing hot pain began within the center of my palm.

I screamed in agonizing pain. My hand retracted from the door handle, and I looked at the palm of my hand to find an upside-down cross burned into my flesh . . . the devil's cross.

My screams emanated out into the breaking dawn. Creaking sounds from within the cathedral quickly led to the door being opened by a short and balding priest. The stiffness of his starched collar and the flat line of his mouth gave him a somber appearance. His penetrating gaze made me extremely nervous.

"Hello, my name is Father Franz, how may I be of help?" he asked.

Before I could respond, something else took over my body. I held up the inside of my palm while small traces of smoke were still secreting out of it. My throat viciously tightened every time I physically tried to communicate.

An entity residing within me refrained my vocal cords from producing any nuance of a sound. Gripping my hands to my throat, I could not move my vocal cords . . . they were completely frozen. I realized to my own horror that I had currently turned mute, but certainly not deaf.

I manifested no phrases at all, something ensconced me in complete silence. As the sky turned pitch-black above us, hundreds of mesmerizing, ebony-feathered ravens began circling the sky above the priest and myself. With the flapping and squawking noises from the ravens above, I almost felt enchanted by the absolute darkness, their various feathers still circling in the now foreboding sky.

Well, everyone knows that the tragically beautiful and majestic raven is actually a message, a carrier, an absolute bringer of . . . death!

In complete shock from the ravens, images of them and other horrors in my mind's eye, a vicious seizure quickly took over my body. Something innate with the center of my being suggested I might not make it through this alive.

After an extremely violent convulsion, I smacked the pavement hard with the left side of my head. My vision ebbed to a murderous black as the ravens circled above. Before I could react, I succumbed to unconsciousness.

Chapter Two

UNANSWERED QUESTIONS

The next day . . .

Stabbing pains from within the left region of my head brought me in and out of consciousness for several hours. Once, in the realm between reality and a world full of dreams, I felt a warm breath against my ear. I shuddered at the mere thought of anything that close to me . . . a strange entity wanting to know more of me than I was willing to reveal. It was a female, benign entity, but what she said left chills shivering up and down my spine.

"Your time has drawn to a near close, and the end of your existence is near . . . for all of those that oppose the holy trinity shall be sent without undue haste into the abysses of the ninth circle in hell." Without warning, a semitransparent feather from some strange entity I could not lucidly discern brushed against my face, only to have a second warm breath against my ear.

"What God has in store for you might not be something to be taken for granted . . . Desdemona."

I bolted out of my bed in sheer terror. Hearing my sounds of utter anguish, an older woman ran into the room for immediate help.

"What seems to be the problem? I heard so much screaming from this room . . . I really hope you're not planning to hurt yourself again," said the woman, with legitimate concern strewn all over her face.

"What the hell is going on?"

"Well, how else did you get the cross cut into your palm?" asked the older woman, then she continued with her speech. "Sorry, my name is Dr. Bennett."

Approximately middle-aged, she had a very stern yet regal presence. She had salt-and-pepper hair, but you could tell she was more agile than the younger resident beside her. Broad shoulders gave her a commanding presence, even though the overall countenance was extremely feminine.

"This is my resident, Dr. Adams, who is studying at this facility."

"Fa . . . fa . . . facility? What are you talking about?" I had a nervous tremor at the mere thought of not understanding everything happening to me.

"Where am I? Who are you people?" While I was looking around in confusion, I noticed a crucifix placed on the wall straight across from my bed.

Internally, I felt disgust and disbelief in the pit of my stomach. Staring at the crucifix, I noticed something strange. Violently, the crucifix moved by itself. I slightly turned my head sideways. The crucifix was turning while shaking uncontrollably against the wall. It finally halted to rest as an upside-down cross. Several violent tremors and shakes made the cross hit the ground with a heavy thud sound that chillingly resonated within the entire room.

Soul-piercing screams from Dr. Bennett and her resident filled the entire room with an unsettling dread. Quickly turning toward them, I screamed, "Where the hell am I? I would like a thorough explanation. Now!" I bellowed at both of them. Feelings of dread began to fester inside my body, igniting my rage held deep within me.

Moments of silence that seemed like an eternity passed between everyone in the room. Finally, Dr. Bennett gave me her entire explanation.

"Sorry about the confusion, but you are currently in a mental health facility." She paused for a moment to collect her thoughts.

"Now," she said, turning to the resident, "In your honest opinion, do you believe that this patient needs any restraints at this current time?"

"No, since she appears to be in no apparent hostile emotional state . . . not required."

Looking back at me, Dr. Bennett continued, "Because of your self-inflicted wounds, Father Franz found it of the utmost urgency to admit you into our care."

Breaking through a moment of silence, I finally spoke. "That's the entire problem I'm currently having with you. I didn't self-inflict the wound on the palm of my hand. The cathedral door burned it into my flesh . . . I just need to figure out the reasons why this occurred."

They looked down toward the floor, as with no eye contact, they could avoid answering my question.

Seething, furious rage boiled from deep within, but my overall cool demeanor on the outside hid what true feelings I actually possessed. Complete disgust and hatred was boiling over for both of the health workers. Why did they not believe me? Accusations of mental instability? I was about to show them some type of mental instability if they would not believe what I was trying to explain.

Dr. Bennett began again. "The injury on your hand did not appear from nothing . . . something caused the injury on your hand . . . why lie? See, it's your misconception of not being able to differentiate between reality and what is obviously not. When you arrive at this realization, of what you did to yourself and why it was wrong, we will talk again."

With the most proper etiquette ever imagined on this forsaken earth, I crudely gave her the middle finger.

As quickly as they had entered the room, they left it to attend to another patient.

My rage had not subsided. My usually pale face became a crimson one full of hatred toward both of the doctors that had left. Confused and alone, I was left to stew in my own juices. Puzzled about my current situation, I felt more like an evil foreign entity was slowly taking me over . . . but what exactly? I realized the freedom I currently lacked was freaking me out. I might as well acclimate myself to the health facility. If I was a patient in a mental health facility, I might as well play the psychotic role that they were so desperately needing. I was already admitted, so I might as well fit in somehow with the other mentally ill patients.

Emotions of anger and hate came and went, then I finally found myself in the only comfort I could actually find—the solitude and black emptiness that thickly covered my dreams as I heavily slept throughout the rest of that day and into the night.

Later that next day, Adam the resident came to talk to me while a nurse administered several pills inside a small, clear plastic cup.

"This should ease the pain a bit. You did suffer a concussion when your head hit the pavement," he said, with legitimate concern evident on his face.

I had almost completely forgotten that had occurred, but my last fleeting memory was the ebony-feathered ravens that had flown above me, almost to take flight later toward another realm. Mystically not observable to the average human being.

Without hesitation, I snatched the pills the nurse handed me and swallowed the entire contents within the clear plastic cup.

"Sure you don't need any water with that?" she asked.

"No" was the only response that I could possibly utter. After my quick ingestion of all my pills, the nurse left the room. Adam sat at my side on a chair. I wished I could escape this prison that I was currently ensconced within, even if my position was only temporary.

Chapter Three

UNEXPECTED MEETING
FROM A DIVINE SOURCE

Seconds turned into minutes, minutes turned into what seemed like an unbearable eternity . . . then Adam left. After that, no one visited me. Before silence became even more unbearable, footsteps finally made their way toward the outer entrance of my room.

Creaking sounds from the door hinge gave way to an intense force to be reckoned with, and his presence was dead center in my room. Afraid of the priest already, I nervously shifted my weight in the chair I was currently sitting in at the table.

"Hello, do you remember me? My name is Father Franz, and I am in today to have a small chat with you."

"Mind if I sit down?" he asked as he looked around the stark-white, almost vacant-looking room. He didn't wait for an answer and sat down across from me at the dark mahogany table.

"Yeah, I mind, but you're going to do what you want anyhow," I snottily retorted.

Ignoring my demeanor, he regarded me quietly, trying to analyze my behavior in as small amount of time as humanly possible.

"Well, if you're checking to see whether I'm dead, I believe the telltale signs are right in front of you," I said this I simultaneously leaned toward him, inches away from his face. He cocked his head sideways. *Not afraid? You should be priest!* I thought.

I whispered in a menacing tone, "Go away . . . before they arrive at your doorstep . . ."

Why was I so furious? Honestly, I had no idea . . .

"What are you talking about?" asked Father Franz defiantly. "I am concerned for you. Have you been administered any medication yet?"

Suddenly, something out of my control happened. Someone or something else was controlling my mind. Through my furious anger and my macabre mental thoughts and imagery, it all happened rather quickly to the unsuspecting priest.

He was screaming uncontrollably, and his sounds of anguish could be heard by the bored receptionist down the hall. Thin walls aided in the receptionist clearly hearing the priest, events that later led to his sheer terror, due to a rather ghastly sight in the near future. The receptionist picked up the phone to alert help.

Retracting his hand, he discovered one word burned into the flesh of his palm . . .

Tragedy.

Screaming in pain, eyes narrowed, he opened the door. He quickly crossed himself as he ran out of the room. Moments later, he sprinted past the receptionist.

"Are you all right, Father? What seems to be the problem?" Almost semi-rising from her chair, she had a look of concern mixed with curiosity placed candidly upon her face.

"Call the doctor," was all he said, as he rushed to a sink to run cold water over his wounded hand.

Then he continued sprinting toward the exit of the mental health ward to make his great escape from what he deemed to be demonic forces at hand. He made his way to the door and quickly turned the handle. Waves of uneasiness and nausea ebbed away to nothing as he was greeted by the warm, fresh breeze, which seemed to flow not only on but through Father Franz's very own vulnerable soul.

"Peace at last!" he declared out loud after escaping what he now knew to be an actual demonic presence that was menacingly hidden within the young woman.

Peace at last . . . or so Father Franz decided to believe at that moment in time.

Chapter Four

MACABRE SKY

Without warning, the sky began to slowly turn into a macabre midnight color. What an odd occurrence, given that it was in the middle of the sunniest part of the afternoon. Glancing at the ominous black entity in the sky, Father Franz noticed that it seemed to be moving in a circular formation. Several seconds passed before he realized that what was in the sky was not an ominous black hole placed above him but a more sinister and foreboding presence—a presence that seemed mesmerizing to witness but seriously held a deadly undertone to the blackened sky. It seemed odd that it had manifested in only mere moments.

What happened next was incomprehensible. It seemed a piece of that black, moving fabric in the sky eventually broke apart. Hundreds of ebony feathers fell down from the sky to suddenly reveal what was actually manifesting above the priest . . . birds. One of the feathers even caressed the right side of his cheek, yet the touch of that exact feather sent violent shivers running up and down his spine. He held up his cross in silent protest to the entire scene—ravens to be exact, with their ebony feathers gleaming in the sun. Their sharp beaks and even sharper talons gave way to a more sinister intention that they might illicit upon the priest.

One by one, hundreds of ravens started to swoop down upon the already unnerved and anxious priest. Talons displayed in a fierce clawlike grip, while their sharp beaks began to make one tumultuous, shrill cry into the newly created, pitch-black, sinister heavens. They were the possible macabre warning that someone would soon end up perished on this forsaken earth, and unfortunately, the one who would literally end up perished was going to be from a more divine source . . . the priest himself.

"No, please. God save me from this menacing presence. Don't let these be my last few precious moments of life." Before he could even utter one more word . . .

Tragedy.

Sharpened beaks and blackened claws began tearing and gouging away at the flesh of the priest. Shrieking in glee as they seemed to wreak havoc upon his body, one raven was even so bold as to take his sharpened beak into his left cornea, plucking his eye out like a mere grape, a piece of fruit that meant nothing to him. A popping sound was the only way his ears were aware that the sadistic raven had taken his eye out of his socket. Well, that and the agonizing pain that accompanied it, of course. Lying almost lifeless on the cold pavement, he could have sworn that he felt a warm breath against his ear whispering a single word: *Tragedy.* He thought that one of the ravens had whispered in his ear. Was it from one of the ravens? Or was he slowly being driven insane? Seconds after the bloodbath and aftermath, the ravens scattered southward. Still, one raven decided to fly a very different route. Now the oily black feathers were glistening crimson from the splattered blood that was scattered on the raven, almost looking like some macabre work of art.

Flying high, the raven finally rested upon the windowsill of Desdemona's room at the mental health facility. The newest inducted woman to date, she stayed in isolation. The upside-down cross burned into the palm of her flesh had led to many varying suspicions by staff members working at the facility. As the raven sat resting on her windowsill, it slowly turned to look her dead in the face.

A moment passed between them. The raven stared at Desdemona not with cruel intent but rather a sort of curiosity as to what entity may be trying to communicate with her. Out of nowhere, Desdemona suddenly felt very groggy and sleepy. Before long, sleep took over her entire being. On dreams of a whisper, she quietly said one word: "Tragedy."

Without hesitation, the raven took flight, since his job has been achieved . . . for now.

Why the receptionist took so long to make the discovery of the priest, only God himself could reveal. After a while, curiosity took control over her, and she cautiously made her way toward the main entrance. Swinging the door wide open, she then reluctantly took several tentative steps outside the building. To her unfortunate discovery, she found the priest lying on the cement pavement, blood pooling heavily underneath his body.

"Father Franz is dead! No . . . God why is this happening? Someone just murdered a priest! Help! Somebody please help me!"

Her screams of sheer terror echoed down the various passageways and side alleys in the city. Still, her screams for the beloved priest did not go in vain. Quickly, Dr. Bennett and her intern, Adam, rushed over for immediate assistance. At this most tragic moment in time, Adam began to have a complete meltdown, since he was from a very Catholic bringing.

"He's dead! Someone murdered a priest! Murder is a sin, but to murder a priest? Unforgivable! May the miscreant, filthy human rot in hell for all eternity . . ."

"Adam, *stop*! You're a professional here! What's next? Having a breakdown in front of a patient? God, that's all we need! Where is your sense of control? Control your emotions *now*! All right, we need to stay calm, cool, and collected if we want to help Father Franz. In his honor, it shall be done," said Dr. Bennett, while soothingly grabbing him by the shoulders for reassurance.

He quietly hugged Dr. Bennett while sobbing uncontrollably in her reassuring embrace. Before long, onlookers began to curiously start walking up to them, asking if they were in need of any assistance.

A bolder individual, in the current sea of onlookers, stepped closely toward the dead priest to take pictures and poke and prod him.

Furious, Adam shoved the bold onlooker away from the dead priest. "How dare you?" he said in a fit of absolute rage. "Don't you have any common sense? Show some respect for the man . . . he's a priest for Christ's sake!" Adam was so furious that his crimson face was giving way to something a bit more menacing, if the bold onlookers would not just mind their own business. After Adam's outburst, he walked directly into the crowd and vanished, never to be seen or heard from ever again.

While the altercation between Adam and the bold onlooker was taking place, Dr. Bennett had called 9-1-1 for an emergency ambulance to pick up the priest. Unfortunately, in reality, she should have bought an obituary in the papers and an undertaker to help with the priest's slain body that lay mere inches away from her feet.

Chapter Five

STRANGE EMOTIONS FROM AN EVEN STRANGER WITNESS

Mere seconds later, a tall woman on top of a snowy mountain peak peered down from her perch high above all the chaos that had ensued below. With enhanced vision beyond that of any ordinary human, she spotted the dead priest that lay on the harsh and unforgiving pavement. Suddenly, her hidden translucent wings spread out into her full wingspan. With the harsh reality that someone within her realm had died, one word creeped into her conscious mind.

Tragedy.

Saddened by the tragic event that she witnessed, she soon succumbed to huge tears of pain and resentment. Uncontrollable emotions led her to cry for even longer than she had anticipated.

With her sorrow and tears, a change in the weather occurred.

Without warning, due to her tears of sorrow, it began to rain.

As the rain fell down upon everyone, Adam and the bold onlooker's altercation had by then fizzed out and subsided to nothing.

Dr. Bennett announced, "All right, Adam, I have an umbrella in my car two feet from here. Go inside now, where you can remain safe and dry." She said this all while calmly walking

Upon the command, Adam quickly did as he was told and hurried back inside the facility.

Moments later, sirens wailed out their own specific cry of distress as they arrived at the tragic and most unfortunate incident. Rushing out with a stretcher, two tall, heavyset men set out toward the priest. One of the men actually bent down to check the priest's pulse, but to no avail, as there wasn't one. His death, this man knew, was not to be taken for granted. His death would not be in vain, not in the slightest.

Regretfully looking to Dr. Bennett, he announced, "Sorry, Dr. Bennett, but this priest is most unfortunately deceased. Although, if you didn't already know, it was not a human that caused his death but an animal instead."

"Animal? What kind would complete such a horrendous act?"

"Well, due to the clawlike marks on his face and throat, accompanied with the gouging in his left eye and throat, I have arrived at a conclusion."

"What is your conclusion, sir?"

"Bird of some sort . . . predatory . . . possibly an enormous flock of them, to complete this sort of tragic result."

The rain outside calmly subsided and gave way to several rays of sun, held high overhead. Mostly, the sun shone toward a mountain peak that rested about a hundred feet away from the macabre incident.

After the medical assistants had wheeled the priest away, they later ended up calling the coroner and heard the tragic news. Dr. Bennett decided to give the bad news of the priest's unfortunate demise to Desdemona. Hurriedly, she stepped inside Desdemona's room to announce what had happened outside the building.

Upon entering, Dr. Bennett witnessed Desdemona staring out the window upon the tragic incident that had recently occurred outside.

Forgetting about the exact trajectory the patient could see, Dr. Bennett finally came to the realization that Desdemona was a possible witness to what had horrifically occurred to the holy man of the cloth.

"I'm afraid you already know what happened, young lady," stated Dr. Bennett calmly.

Slowly turning her head, Desdemona looked Dr. Bennett dead in the eye. Only one word was uttered from her, in a creepy hiss with her tone of voice: "Tragedy."

A moment of eerie silence passed between them. Finally, Desdemona confessed a small piece of her innermost true intentions.

"Watching the priest die was the best thing that ever happened to me, it almost felt . . . surprisingly . . . refreshing."

The toxic fumes of her words emitted toward Dr. Bennett, as if they were a poison.

"How dare you say that! What an awful confession to make, and of an actual priest, to make matters worse! You should be ashamed of yourself! You're *pure* evil!" yelled Dr. Bennett as she scolded Desdemona for her cruelly intended comments.

Dr. Bennett turned to leave the room, only for Desdemona to quickly let out another creepy utterance of vile commentary. Covering up her left eye with her left hand, Desdemona yelled out to Dr. Bennett, "Don't lose sight of what lies ahead. this is only the beginning!"

Dr. Bennett briskly walked away and calmly shut the entrance door behind herself. Suddenly, a noise seemed to fill up the room—it was actually the noise of evil laughter.

The laughter, with its evil, macabre essence, emanated into the entire room, almost echoing among the very walls it inhabited.

Tragedy, well, Desdemona's reaction was a sinister laugh that filled up the entire room, like some sinister entity with evil intent trying to make its way into our own reality through her sinister laughter.

Chapter Six

BLOODBATH

The following day, a female orderly walked in to administer a simple "birdie bath" as she called it, to make sure Desdemona was up to par with their strict code on health and sanitization levels regimented by the facility.

Unwrapping a crisp, folded-up, white terry cloth, she proceeded with administering the cleansing regimen. At first, everything was normal, and Desdemona was already wrapped in a larger white terry towel for modesty. Suddenly, something strange began to appear on the cloth. It seemed as if the cloth was slowly changing into a different color, so the orderly slowly began to ring out the cloth. Wringing it out with a heavy twist, she saw slow droplets of crimson-red blood fall into the cleansing bowl, morphing its contents from water into blood.

Startled by the overall change, the orderly screamed out with a fearful tone in her voice. "Help, help, we need some assistance over here! ASAP! Please, one of our patients needs immediate attention!" Without hesitation, Dr. Bennett emerged through the door, flinging it wide open to inspect what was occurring in the patient's room.

"What seems to be the problem? Oh my God, did she lose that much blood from her body? Is she regressing to cutting herself again?" Panicked concern had taken over the facial features of the head superintendent to the facility.

"That's the whole point, Dr. Bennett, she didn't cut herself at all. The water in the cleansing bowl changed all of a sudden into blood," said the orderly, with a hint of fear in her voice, afraid to hear the doctor's final reaction to her current comment.

"You're joking, right? You think it's fun and games dealing with *this* patient?" asked Dr. Bennett.

"No, I'm being completely serious with you, Dr. Bennett. If you thoroughly examine her, you will find no cuts, bruises, or markings of any kind." She slowly held up her hands to show some mockery of a submissive defeat.

"I don't know, Doctor, never saw water turn into blood until today. Sorry, just thought you should be made aware." With that said, she hurried out of the room before anything stranger occurred.

After a five-minute, thorough inspection by the doctor, no markings of any kind were identified on the patient's body, and there were no identifying marks of any kind on Desdemona. Actually, quite the opposite seemed to be happening. It almost seemed that Desdemona was not bleeding but actually morphing or changing her skin. Her pale skin seemed smoother than before and completely blemish-free, yet *cold* and clammy. When Dr. Bennett checked her pulse, there was not one to even discover on the patient.

Desdemona again looked her dead in the eye and whispered creepily, "Still alive, you just can't tell all the time, Doctor."

Without hesitation, Dr. Bennett fled the room, calling for her intern, Adam, to quickly assist her in the bizarre matter. *Bizarre shit.*

Still, the next day arrived, and nothing out of the ordinary happened. A week passed, then two, until a whole month passed without any bizarre situations happening at all with Desdemona. After a while, it seemed as if life would be finally restored to some semblance of normalcy for the young woman. Well, minus the macabre upside-down cross burned deep into her flesh. It still remained on the inside of her left hand, as a silent reminder of what lurked beneath her innermost being . . . a demon residing, or actually slumbering, within her. With its own sinister malice, this demon had latched on to her very own vulnerable soul, only to wreak havoc again at a later time.

Chapter Seven

RELEASING THE DEMON

Finally, the day arrived when Desdemona was ready to be released out into the world. But would the world be ready for Desdemona? With the tragic events that had already happened in the past, how would the young woman keep her mind balanced in the aftermath? Well, knowing the fact that she didn't mind what happened to the priest, or almost reveled in his demise, was rather devastating to witness from a mental health perspective. Still, Desdemona did have one final check-in before she was released from the mental health facility.

Brought in carefully by Dr. Bennett's intern, Adam, Desdemona gingerly took her seat across from the superintendent. With all the strength she could muster, Desdemona willed herself to remain calm. With red plastic glasses placed at the bridge of her nose and eyes gazing down to meet her, Dr. Bennett began. "All right, young lady, I am going to ask you a series of questions. How you answer them will determine whether you will stay here or have the freedom to leave this facility," said Dr. Bennett, with stress in her voice.

"Given previous circumstances with you, actually, you're lucky this final check-in is even occurring today."

Time had nearly stopped for Desdemona when she heard Dr. Bennett utter the words *freedom to leave this facility.*

Regaining her composure, she thought of many manipulative ways that she could quickly gain her much-needed freedom . . . now in her mind, the wheels were all set in motion.

"First, do you admit to actually cutting yourself on the palm of your left hand?" asked the doctor.

"Yes, Dr. Bennett, but I made up the story as a means to get attention from people since I was currently homeless and escaping an abusive relationship. I currently have no working income as well—he was that controlling of me. I was thinking of a resolution, not thinking that all these events would happen and I would wind up here."

"Well, there are better ways to reach out to people instead of cutting yourself, Desdemona," said Dr. Bennett sternly.

"I agree now, but I was really desperate at the time, and I was in need of some attention," said Desdemona, with a surprisingly cool overall demeanor.

"Next question. What you said about the priest . . . that cryptic confession that you delivered to me . . . do you have any remorse?" asked Dr. Bennett.

"At first, no, Doctor, but then I gave myself a moment to think things through that day. Yet again, if I get enough attention, hey . . . I still get a roof over my head and out of an abusive relationship. I know that sounds terrible, but you have to understand where I am coming from, Doctor."

"Oh, and where are you coming from exactly?" asked the doctor.

"From an abusive relationship. I ran to the Catholic church to escape my abusive boyfriend! I remember the very last thing that he said to me," Desdemona continued.

"'Just you and me . . . let's have some fun together' my boyfriend whispered in my ear, as he pressed a Colt .45 to the left side of my head. My abusive boyfriend also said the same line before he burned a cigar out on my left shoulder. That was a month ago, before I ran to the cathedral on the day he threatened to take my life with his brand-new katana that he specially had handcrafted and shipped from Japan."

A moment of silence passed between them.

"Really? Well, emotionally that explains a lot. So, the case here is that you were causing fair amounts of drama to only end up getting provided protection from your abusive boyfriend? Please, Desdemona, reach out to a professional like myself or someone else. You don't need to get into theatrics. I will always provide help for you whenever it's needed."

"You're absolutely right, Doctor. Looking back on it, I do see the error of my ways.'"

"Confessing you actually know the difference between right and wrong is very reassuring to me, so Desdemona, I am going to discharge you from this facility. You may leave at the end of the day, sometime this afternoon before 5:00 p.m."

Gathering up her final forms to give to the receptionist, she briskly walked out of the room.

Freedom by the end of today? A small smirk began to play on Desdemona's lips, only to quickly disappear when the intern, Adam, entered the room.

"All right, Desdemona, I am here to take you back to your room for the last time. Your release from this facility commences this afternoon. Good luck, Desdemona."

"Thank you, Adam, this means the world to me," Desdemona said as she quickly passed him to return to her room for the final time.

Several hours passed, and her freedom finally arrived. Dr. Bennett and Adam wished her well, and she was finally on her way.

Upon exiting the mental health facility, a light breeze swept across her pale face and through her raven-black hair. She finally inhaled her first breath of fresh air, which had not occurred for the past two months. Having to be locked away like she was in some sort of prison was very upsetting to her. Truly, the prison she inhabited already consumed her heart, her soul, and her mind.

Almost as if some evil spirit was inhabiting her body yet taking control over it all in one overwhelming instance.

A small smile displayed on her lips as she whispered, "Tragedy."

Everything that she had told Dr. Bennett had absolutely been a lie. Manipulative tactics must be enacted if she was to have her freedom, and now it finally came to pass. The part about her abusive boyfriend was completely untrue. Instead, he was probably just lying in their bathtub taking a nice, relaxing bath. Maybe a little too relaxing. With his slit throat, she seriously doubted he would be going anywhere at the moment. Killing him was an exhilarating experience, from his blissful nap in the tub, the initial shock when he felt the steel-cold blade at his throat. The blood was all she could remember at that time. Oh, all of that thick, oozing, crimson-red blood.

Chapter Eight

GRAVEDIGGER COMPANIONS

Having a couple of gravedigger friends who worked at the local funeral home helped me out a lot during my dire, most cumbersome circumstance at the time. Also, knowing them since high school, years ago, was beneficial as well. Their names were Wayne and Trent, and back in the day, they said that if I ever needed help, they would be there for me. The time for their much-needed help was now. To dispose of my decaying boyfriend's remains.

Late at night, my friends would clean up the bloody mess that I created and would dispose of his body in a remote location—somewhere in the mountains, a few hundred feet from where I lived. While they were being the "cleaners," I would be busy calling up friends and family, announcing that we were finally going to take a flight out toward Milan, Italy. We always wanted to take the trip, but we never got around to actually going to Italy. That should hold them off for about two months, which was supposed to be the duration that we would both be spending in that country.

Several hours later, the time drew near to meet up with my friends in the mountains. Upon my arrival, my friends exchanged glances and then drew back so that I could inspect their work— the freshly made burial plot that they had only mere seconds ago completed for me. Cautiously peering down into the unmarked burial plot, I discovered to my own initial shock that my boy-friend was already lying at the bottom of it. Arms crossed over each other upon his chest, his hands actually covered the grue-some slashes from when I had no control over myself at the time. Some other entity had completely taken me over, and all I felt now finally . . . was nothing. Viewing him now in his deceased form, the finality of it hit me hard, like some freight train had just run over my body at full tilt.

Shaking my head to get that image out of my mind, I walked over to one of the shovels and swung one over my left shoulder. Grinning ear to ear at both of my friends, I announced, "All right, guys, time to bury the tragic bastard that abused me for so many years. Let's throw some dirt on this already dirty *tragedy* of a man."

Shoveling the heavy sodded dirt on top of him with fierce determination, I felt absolutely no remorse at all. No feelings of sorrow, resentment, pain, or even anger. Knowing my cool detachment about the entire situation was not the wisest thing to show, I immediately bent my head down and quickly pro-ceeded to work beside my two friends. An hour later, I was wip-ing the sweat off my brow and contemplating a peaceful night's rest after shoveling all the mounds of dirt that were needed to cover up his remains.

"All right, let's throw some branches and twigs over this mound of dirt to give it a more natural appearance. After that, we are out of here." Wayne made a circling motion with his hand as if to say, *That's a wrap folks, we're done for the night.* After a few minutes of working on a more naturalistic overall look, the three of us departed from the area. Since I had nowhere else to go, I stayed with them for the night, since they happily lived in a remote location that was far from the city limits.

Flying swiftly from a sunset sky, a tall, benign entity quickly appeared perched on top of the deceased man's grave site. Translucent wings spread out around the grave, completely covering it in some semblance of a protective act toward the now deceased individual. Laying her hand on top of the mound of dirt, she whispered one word: "Justice." Sure, he may have been a horrible individual, but there was no right in taking the life of another, without any repercussions at all to your own life.

A few minutes passed, and then the entity began to look toward the heavens. It would be dark soon, and that was certainly no time for any of her kind to be lurking around in the mountains. It just wasn't a safe enough environment. Before the time carried on, she took flight toward the heavens, sadly coming to the realization that she had much work to do before her return.

An hour later, I told my best friends Wayne and Trent good night and made my way toward the guest bedroom. Fatigue quickly took over my entire body, and I fell on top of the mattress with my face looking out toward the window. Before my dreams took me out of the grim reality of everything that I was dealing with, I noticed something very peculiar. Translucent wings from some sort of tall, birdlike entity was flying in the sky. The speed alone was swift enough to know that it was predatory . . . but for some odd reason, I felt for the first time in my life that I one day could possibly end up being the prey, instead of the mean, predatory entity that I longed to become in my own personal life. On dreams of a whisper, I heard one word before I drifted off to sleep. *Justice*.

The next day, I was eating some breakfast with my friends and mulling over everything that happened last night. Smells of flavorful sugar-cured ham, maple-syrup-drenched pancakes, and scrambled eggs with cheese in them, filled the air in an almost homely atmosphere that made everything else from last night seem surreal. Still, looking back on the past events from last night, I could only selfishly contemplate my own departure from this area by the end of the week. Maybe I would take one last visit to view my ex-boyfriend lying dead and buried in his grave. Ignorantly, I evilly contemplated pissing on his grave before leaving this European country forever. The United States might be nice. Hell, I could reside in Salem, Massachusetts—the area sounded right up my alley.

Chapter Nine

A DEMONIC FORCE ENCOUNTERING THE LORD'S DIVINE

After the excellent breakfast, we all said our goodbyes, and I was on my way to start my drastic escape plan. Better now than never, I had previously told my friends during breakfast. They had been so adamant about me "lying low" and staying with them for at least a week. No, my instincts were telling me to leave now, and I knew listening to my intuition was the best thing to do for someone in my current position. Exiting their home, I realized that without them, I was truly more alone in this world than I had ever been before in my entire life. Shrugging these insecurities aside, I carried on to get some much-needed shopping done so I could later make my great escape. Just the essentials—anything more would simply raise suspicion. At this time more than ever, being "noticed" by authority or anyone else was something I could simply not afford.

Putting all of my essentials in a convenient brown canvas backpack, it seemed impossible to gather everything I needed in such a short amount of time. Instincts again were telling me that my time was limited. I was not about to squander what precious time I had before my departure. Outside, the weather had changed drastically. Rain pouring down in heavy torrents and heavy winds from the east gave an appearance of the weather providing an ominous tone of what was to quickly arrive in the near future.

Quickly grabbing my phone, I called for the nearest taxi service to come and take me to my next destination. Already knowing that I had another friend, named Jamal, to help me out with my current situation, was also a very nice reassurance. Approximately twenty minutes later, Jamal showed up with his cab to give me a lift. Wishing that I had an umbrella, I silently scolded myself for not remembering such a basic necessity.

A moment of silence passed between us.

Suddenly, before I had barely shut the cab door, we were already driving off to my destination. Also being able to tell him where I was going before he even arrived was very beneficial. For a moment, something strange began to occur on my seat. It felt as if I had sat in something very mushy and wet, and the entire stench was too unbearable to take any longer.

Quickly, I asked Jamal, "Hey, why does it stink back here? I feel like I just sat in something terrible."

A smirk slowly played on his lips before he retorted, "Oh yeah, forgot to mention, the last person that sat in the back seat was an older lady that suffered from complete incontinence. So, you're probably setting in her bodily fluids right now." He said this so matter-of-factly that he might as well have been stating the weather forecast for the night.

"Don't be shy, just come out and say it . . . I just sat in some piss and shit, and there are no holds barred on the laughter right now," I stated with a look of utter embarrassment strewn all over my pale countenance.

"You got that right. Sorry, I never would have thought to check the back seat."

Then he let out laughter that emanated so loudly that the entire universe could probably hear the sound. In secret, I was selfishly wondering whether he just left the mess there to see my initial reaction. Letting the window that separated us slide to the left, he handed me a box of Kleenex and a trash bag. Silently, he was making the suggestion of completing a quick cleanup, which I knew I desperately needed at the time. After the mess was taken care of, he turned around and handed me a spraying air freshener to get the putrid stench out of the air. A few minutes later, everything was back to normal minus the back seat of my pants where I had hastily taken my seat. About fifteen minutes later, we finally arrived at my destination. We were located at the bottom of the mountain, approximately two feet from where I previously buried my boyfriend's remains. Nervously, I handed him my cab fare, and he held up his hand in a silent gesture as if to imply, "Hey, we have been friends for *way* too long . . . this one's on me, Desdemona."

"All right, guess this is it for me. Hope to see you sometime in the near future."

Why I made the comment, I will never know, because it made absolutely no sense whatsoever. I felt as if someone was watching me in secret, their eyes penetrating into my soul-less body and saying, "Wow, you are one cold, ruthless . . . the rest you can figure out for yourself. Without any hesitation, I made my way up the two-mile stretch where my ex-boyfriend's remains lay buried. Luckily, the rain had subsided, but it by no means gave way to any light filtering from above. Too cloudy to produce the brightest rays of sun, I felt as if I was emotionally drained and the weather was only a mere reflection of what my true emotions were producing at this time.

Walking uphill, I almost thought that my feet could not carry me any farther after one mile, but I still dauntingly had another one to complete. Dredging on, the weight of my backpack was too much for me to handle. Easing the cumbersome backpack off my shoulders, I gingerly set it down to inspect what I could possibly eat at the time, as slight fatigue had taken over my entire body. Stress could trigger many emotions, but it could also sink its talons into the flesh of even physical pain. At least in my shoulder region, that was the true source of my pain at the time. Inside the backpack, I discovered several things that I did not initially intend to buy at the store. Useless items such as a waffle maker and ground coffee were in my bag, for reasons even unknown to myself. As ruthless and cold as I could be about things in life in general, you would have figured some entity out there in the world should have gifted me with the overall talents of logic of practical matters. Alas, that was really not my forte, and at least I would be honestly willing to admit that, even if it was only said to myself in secret.

Finding a delicious-looking bag of trail mix, I ripped the bag open and almost poured half the contents into my wide, gaping mouth. After a few minutes, my hunger subsided, and I rubbed my shoulders to make sure there was no hypertension. Feeling none at the time, I rested my backpack on top of my shoulders and carried on with my hiking adventure. About fifteen minutes later, I finally set my backpack down close by his burial plot that my friends and I so lovingly had made. Oh, the fond memories that I could possibly describe to everyone . . . the time he threatened to take my life for looking at him the wrong way. Also, there was the sweet revenge that he got on me by handcuffing me to one of the pipes that held the water heater in our place to teach me a lesson for staying after work an extra hour without notifying him. Literally, my duration next to the water heater was exactly seven hours, twenty-one minutes, and two seconds. Yes, my time was exact, due to the fact that my watch was still placed on my left wrist.

Luckily, I didn't have work that day or there would have been calls placed by them that would have elicited more severe abusive attempts in my direction. What fond memories. Quickly unzipping my pants and pulling them down slightly, I began to take a gigantic piss on top of his grave. Wow, revenge sure was sweet when it was done in just the right way to make it a really memorable moment.

Near the top of the mountain peak, enormous translucent wings spread out to cover up the body that was cleansing itself by a nearby stream. Washing her face thoroughly, she looked up from her cleansing to encounter the foulest smell the universe had ever bestowed upon this unforsaken earth. Unfortunately, the wretched stench entered her ultrasensitive nostrils.

"Disgusting." That was all she could utter at the moment. Almost retching from the stench, she became curious as to what specific entity could create such a vile smell. Soon, after her bathing was complete, she would find out the exact source of the putrid smell that was now occurring in the lower regions of the mountain.

After pulling my pants up after taking a piss on top of his grave, the mound of buried dirt where my ex-boyfriend resided was now saturated in my heartfelt sentiments of putrid smelling urine. I felt now as if some strange entity of darkness shrouded and surrounded me. It seemed to engulf me in some sort of bizarre form of protection. Still, it was performed in a way that was more of a comfort than something that had any actual malicious intent. Although, as I was contemplating my great escape plan when all of this was occurring, something strange began to appear on the horizon. Gigantic translucent wings spread out to reveal the tallest bird I had ever witnessed in my entire existence. No, wait . . . it wasn't a bird at all, not by any means. Actually, she was an extremely tall woman with a look of heaven, but I highly suspected that she thought nothing but hell toward me. Billowing white hair flowed from her like the clouds from the heavens. I knew this entity, even if it was benign, had some malicious intent to deal out to me. The most striking feature about the woman was her all-white eyes—not from cataracts, or anything of that nature, but from an actual natural appearance . . . as if it was a natural fit she was born with, a birthright. Now I knew what rights she had . . . to the benign, to the heavens, and for whatever was fair and just in this world.

Opening with honesty, even for me, had to spare me some time so that I could possibly escape this entity who, oddly enough, I thought might be one of God's messengers . . . one of his most precious angels sent from on high.

Fucking figures.

With a sinister smirk on my face, I began, "I'm no hero, not by any means, but you have to admit that my ex-boyfriend deserved to die."

The angel had a shocked look on her face and said, "If you were ever free from sin, I would not have to be seeking you out at this present time. You better be smart if you think that for one second you can get away with murder . . . especially one of a priest!"

"How the hell did you realize that happened?" I asked with complete shock written all over my face. Continuing, I said, with an evil smirk on my face, "He deserved it, and by the way, I watched him die." Still, the sinister smirk did not leave my face, not even for a second in time.

"So did I," said the angel. "And I cried for what seemed like an eternity. My sorrow was so immense that it brought on the changing of the weather. My tears literally brought the rain."

"Are you kidding me? Great, do you have the power to part the red seas with your rage too, brought to you by some angelic being from beyond the poor, pitiful part of being a pathetic martyr for Christ? Tell me, angel, when a priest for Christ dies at the hands of the opposition, who's to say what is obviously not going to happen? Justice." Sinister laughter ensued just for that added jab, while that innocent little wretch wished I could be brought down a peg or two.

Before I knew what happened, she let out some type of shriek that almost sent me reeling from the internal pain in my ear canal. While I was dazed and confused, she then lunged at me full tilt and grabbed me by the collar of my T-shirt. Leaning in, only inches away from my face, she whispered, "Don't you *ever* use blasphemy toward the almighty Christ or you will suffer at the hands of a higher being that will not be so benevolent." I had never angered an angel before in my entire life, but I knew that my life might be nearing a close if I made any more drastic remarks. So, I did something else out of the ordinary. Instead, I leaned in closer to her face, took a huge wad of saliva in my mouth, and quickly spat in the face of God's most menacing right-hand assailant.

Not uttering a word, she silently wiped the spit from her face with the back of her hand and said, "You will pay for the crimes committed on that priest, as well as your incompetent ex-boyfriend. This will not be the last time you hear from me . . . Desdemona." Without a word, she spread out her gigantic translucent wings and looked up toward the heavens. A huge beam of radiating white light completely ensconced her, and then she was gone within a blink of an eye. Before another blink of an eye, I was already halfway down to the bottom of the mountain to make my great escape.

Remembering past events, the taxicab was completely out of the question, but walking a decent two miles before pitching an extremely small tent that I bought from the store would be sufficient for me at this time. They always say hell hath no fury like a woman scorned . . . but who's to say what you should do to complete the revenge for who damaged my soul? Hell, after all the abuse I suffered over the years, I knew that I was officially a soulless creature, just doomed to roam this world, forever searching for some semblance of retribution.

An hour later, I began pitching my tent and creating my kindling to complete my campfire, since nightfall would soon be encroaching upon me without a moment's notice. After everything was set, I grabbed some more essential food and munched it up by the glow of the embers that lit up the night sky. The fire seemed to be doing some sacred dance in the night that looked extremely like innocent handmaidens being slowly tortured in the fiery depths of hell. Shaking these thoughts aside, I changed my mind quickly to the warmth of the overall fire. Maybe there was too much kindling, but I needed to stay warm if I was to make it through the night. Luckily, it was springtime instead of winter, so the outdoor elements would not become too harsh on my body. Finally, I called it a night and went in my tent to rest my weary bones from the brutality of God's right-hand man—or woman, for that matter. If *that* was my opposition, I needed all the help I could possibly muster up to fight back.

As the rain fell down upon my tent later in the night, I couldn't help but wonder if it was, in secret, due to an angel off in the distance, counting her many tears of sorrow for the depravity of mankind everywhere. The pitch-black night eventually gave way to a brighter morning, one in which the only person I had to worry about was myself. Hell, at least that way, I knew that I would be protected. Would I be capable of abusing myself physically? Probably not. I had too much to live for . . . and too many things to kill as well.

Chapter Ten

CRAZY TRAIN

Later in the day, I quickly ate again and then packed up my tent for a farther journey south of this location. Luckily, if I could receive some internal strength, it was approximately five miles toward the next train station. Luckily, I had just enough money for one ticket, with enough left over to last me for about two weeks, give or take a day or two.

Most of the day was spent making the hike toward my train stop destination. Awaiting me there would be something so peculiar and out of the ordinary that my mind might not even be able to process it properly. Making stops several times, I felt as if my aching body could not carry on with one more step without passing out from fatigue due to my extensive traveling. Finally, the train station was in front of me, and I took my much-needed rest on one of the benches in the waiting area near where the train dropped and picked up its passengers. Half an hour later, I felt refreshed and new . . . bullshit. At least I got some rest, so I was not feeling completely drained of all my energy. Next, I made my way to the ticket booth and purchased one for myself. Then I heard the unfortunate news. Since I had arrived later in the day, the next train would not arrive until 9:00 a.m. the next business day. They apologized for the inconvenience, and I gave a very unconvincing smile—like I actually gave a damn about them at all.

At least there were restrooms in this area. I quickly went in and quickly cleaned myself up. There was no time for small talk with anyone. Even if I was stuck here, I had no time to lose by saying the wrong thing, at the wrong time, toward the wrong person.

Due to my extensive wait, the price of the ticket was reduced by 50 percent, so I had the advantage of taking over the concession stand for a while. Moments later, I could be seen with yellow mustard dripping down my sunken-in chin, and I quickly wiped the remnants away with a napkin. The pretzel bun was a nice treat, after everything that I had been previously dealing with at the time.

Resting myself again on a beige-painted bench, I was wondering exactly what that angel I encountered last night was doing right now, at this exact moment. Was she talking to God about what vile filth I was to mankind? Was she preening her translucent feathers in angst to prepare to destroy me later in life? Were angels even allowed to aggressively fight us mere mortals? Or did she realize what I truly was . . . which might get me a macabre ticket from the angel herself stating, "You must be dealt with by the Almighty . . . or suffer the dire consequences." With that tragic scenario playing through my mind, I nervously boarded the train, inquisitive as to what might occur the next time that I encountered God's benign lady of the heavens.

Upon boarding the train, I glanced around at the interior that seemed to be quite impressive. Plush, heavily cushioned seats were available for all passengers, with bottles of water in each individual holder for anyone who had an immediate thirst. The flooring had a dark tapestry of carpet with various hues of green and beige woven strategically into it to give it a very heavy yet decadent appearance. Wide, expansive arched glass windows allowed some light to filter into the train that gave it an almost homely atmosphere, if it wasn't for all of the loud passengers clamoring for their numbered specified seats that might tragically vanish if they did not get in their seat within thirty seconds or less.

Taking my seat, I was lucky enough to receive a place positioned beside one of the windows so I could enjoy the vast majority of the hills, valleys, and mountainous terrain. Those mountains . . . what truly was held or hidden within them? I felt as if an entity lived there, one that was not so benign. Instead of killing me outright, it waited in the depths of those mountains to later wreak havoc on every individual that ever had any indiscretions or tragic events they may have created.

As the train moved, I began to brush all of the various worries away from my mind, just to escape my many troubles. Still, in the end, I knew that they would all end up haunting me later in my life, like some sick reminder that never went away, from past misdeeds that could never be corrected. For if death could be corrected, I would have far more problems now than ever before in my entire existence on this unforsaken earth.

Rolling hills and valleys covered the landscape, with various scenes of mountains that I could view off in the distance. Green as an emerald was the terrain, and the train almost seemed like it was rolling through some scene that was just a piece of heaven. Somewhere I was never going to be allowed ever in my existence, not with my previous misdeeds completed. An evil smirk was quickly playing on my lips when I was thinking of that piece of heaven. Then I uttered only one word in a whisper, "Tragedy."

Later that night, shocked out of my slumber, I heard a strange thud directly above me. I quickly got out of my seat to make my way toward the bathroom. Desperately needing to splash some cool water on my face, I turned the bathroom door handle and entered the room. Maybe doing so would finally calm my already unraveled and fraying nerves.

As I entered the bathroom, nothing seemed out of the ordinary. So, I cleansed my face with some mild soap and water. After grabbing a white towel from beside the sink, I proceeded to wipe off excess soap from my face. Before I had accomplished the task, I heard a faint whisper directly above my head.

"Desdemona."

Cautiously looking around the bathroom, I tried to find the exact source of the whispered voice. Beside me, the white towel still clung to the sink, a secretive, soggy reminder that left chills running up and down my spine. Limp, lifeless, and with nothing else to live for, the cloth was now only a physical reminder of how I was internally feeling at this exact moment in time.

A moment of silence passed through the night, like a breeze through the various trees we were all passing by outside the train.

Again, I heard the faint whisper . . . "Desdemona."

Looking up, I noticed a large glass sunroof that was square shaped. Directly above my head, it almost looked crystal clear. Through the glass, I could even see the newly formed dawn of the horizon. As curiosity took over the rest of me, I carefully climbed onto the sink to get a better vantage point as to where the source of the whisper had actually occurred. Getting my face as close to the glass as physically possible, I heard the faint whisper draw near in a slow, more menacing undertone than what was previously heard.

"You're mine, Desdemona."

Startled by the response, I was already too late to protest against anything at all. Pieces of broken glass shards fell all around me with a deafening sound. Before I could even utter a sound, a large hand grabbed me by the scalp of my head and placed me on top of the deadly fast-paced freight train.

Uncertain of what was occurring, I blinked a few times to quickly recover my vision. Shards of glass were buried in my hair, clothes, and anything else that you could possibly imagine. Slowly glancing upward, I noticed the same angel that had appeared to me in the mountains.

Chapter Eleven

A Strange Transformation

"What the hell are you doing?" I asked in a menacing tone. "Well, I have come here to save humanity from a very wretched woman, and you, my dear, are nothing more than a menace to society," said the angel.

"Really? I didn't realize that anything that had to deal with you was something that I was supposed to give a damn about during our second encounter," I said while lifting myself into a standing position.

Feeling the scorn from that comment, the angel began to move in a strange manner. Not quite having an epileptic seizure, she more or less looked like she was doing some type of abstract dance. Flailing her arms about with an overall finale of shuddering convulsions, she surprisingly, to my dismay, began to display a very odd and strange transformation.

The white-haired angel, without any warning, broke apart her body in dozens of different pieces and quickly morphed into several dozens of different mourning doves that took flight into the breaking dawn of the newly created horizon.

Without any time to even put up a decent fight against her, my vision began to blur. Feathers swept against my face in an almost torrent of doves encircling my entire body. Before I could do anything to stop her, she had morphed back into her human form and kidnapped me as she took flight toward the heavens.

Sadly, my heart was truly longing for the pitch-black, macabre night that gave me so much comfort. Now I severely know no comfort at all. Just the torrent of feathers flying around me, trying to extract the very essence of me that made me who I truly was inside . . . pure evil.

Due to the events spiraling out of control, I could no longer see anything in front of me. Everything blurred, and then I quickly ended up passing out due to all of the recent stress from previous events leading up to being strangely kidnapped by an angel . . . but only one that would instead end up torturing me in my own personal hell on this unforsaken earth.

Taken back to wherever this entity called home, I was startled by a heavy thud as I landed on the concrete floor. Instinctively, I knew that this was not going to end well for anyone. First, I had to figure out the exact location that she kidnapped me to, so I could *again* strategize my great escape plan. Slowly looking up, I noticed the angel standing directly over me, not with any anger or malice in her demeanor, but with a look of contempt on her face that would have been more suited for a dirty dog or some other overall subservient entity.

With my own personal look of contempt toward the angel, I menacingly whispered, "The heavy weight in my mind is not from above, you pathetic angel. Watch it!" I said as an evil smirk began to play on my thin lips.

Suddenly, leaning toward my face, stopping only a mere inch way, she said, "If your mind's not from above, I may put you and the rest of your body buried down below, you wretched woman!" Her all-white eyes were glowing, as if someone had just turned on some high beam lights inside her eyeballs to accentuate her already strange overall appearance.

In response to the comment, I viciously spit on the face of God's right-hand liaison. This being would actually end up torturing me, as if she were from a less benevolent place . . . maybe a possible fiery location hidden in the depths of hell.

Fucking figures.

Oh well, hell hath no fury like a woman scorned . . . but did the angel? Realizing that I had been the scorned individual . . . soon, she would quickly discover . . . the changling.

I was imprisoned by this angel, who furiously slammed the door behind her with a click sound of the locking mechanism. The fact that I had just spit in her face may have been a main factor to her quick retreat.

Defeated? Far from it! I was the one who was kidnapped and held prisoner in some type of lackluster minimalistic basement. It was dank, dark, and cold. Essentially, it was the internal composition of me, just thrown into a basic interior room design. Overall, before depression set in due to the décor of the basement, I ended up sleeping on a mattress on the floor that had many various rodents' fecal matter on top of it. Brushing it aside with my hands, I fell asleep, red in the face from being kidnapped by an angel. Damn, seeing that she was an angel, you figure at least the living space here would not be even the slightest bit subpar. Anyway, due to stress and fatigue, I drifted off to sleep.

Chapter Twelve

TRAINING DAY

On macabre dreams from a distant whisper, I almost had a faint memory of one translucent, shimmering white wing sweeping slightly across my left cheek. Someone whispered in my ear, "Desdemona . . . I now own whatever is left of your putrid soul. See this kidnap as your saving grace card. Promise to never kill again and I will free you from this prison."

Frightened, I woke up and stared at the entrance door to the basement. Walking slowly out the door was one thing, but she instead seemed to be floating as she walked, as if she were actually just floating on cloud nine for not being me at all.

Damn, I thought to myself, *I wish I could drown her in a pool. Hell, that would really make her float.*

Shoving all macabre thoughts aside, I finally received some much-deserved rest. Deeply sleeping in an almost comatose slumber, I was suddenly awoken by the angel poking and prodding me with a *gigantic* stick.

"What . . . what time is it?" I asked in a stupefied manner, since I was still groggy and not yet fully awake.

"The time is 6:00 a.m., and we are now in preparation to begin your training."

"Training? What are you talking about?"

"Well, look directly over there," said the angel as she pointed over toward the entrance door.

A sign written above the door read: "Cleanse the Wicked."

Holy shit. They were the only two words I could think of at the time, given everything that was happening to me now.

Envisioning my life flashing quickly before my own vision, I glanced toward the entrance door with the macabre sign above it. As I tried to turn the doorknob, my heart sank heavy within myself. Uneasiness overcame me as I slowly realized that the door had been locked the entire time. No wonder the angel didn't even react to my running toward the door; her plans had been carefully calculated beforehand.

Not knowing where to turn or where to go, I thought of a quick plan. Pretending to be scared, I put my back against the door and then slid slowly down toward the floor to assume the fetal position. My arms were entwined on top of my head as if to say, "Hey, if you strike out at me, at least my arms will be the *ultimate* protection against any weapons you may have in your arsenal . . . you can bet on that!

A moment of silence passed between us in the room.

Finally, she made her way over toward me in a very slow yet methodical manner. Standing over me, she uttered the words, "The first three lessons will be about hearing, seeing, and speaking no evil. The first lesson will begin with speaking no evil, so . . . I have planned on burning the tip of your tongue off!" said the angel in a triumphant, if not psychotic, manner. The entire time that she was talking, I had stayed in the fetal position, with hands now in tight fists to ward her off. Leaning in closer, she retracted a small yet very pristine scalpel. Damn, this angel was not messing around at all . . . figures. A prank was one thing, but this lesson seemed a little too macabre even for someone like me.

As she leaned in toward me to remove my arms from on top of my head, I quickly lunged at her full tilt. Dropping the blade, she let out a short exclamation as she fell to the floor. Reaching out to recover the scalpel resting on the floor, I finally caught my own opportunity. Making a mad dash toward the blade, I quickly scooped it up and sent a crushing blow to my opponent. As her hand was still flayed out there, I viciously stomped on that innocent open hand.

"Aahh!" screamed the angel in agonizing pain. Leaning down to peer at her, only mere inches away from her face, I uttered the words, "Where is your God to save your now, angel?" I said this menacingly with an evil smirk on my face. Saying absolutely nothing, she tried to push and scoot herself with her hands away from me. Absolute shock and terror were written all over her face. Before she could scoot any farther, I grabbed her by both ankles and brought her back over to me. Without clearly thinking, I leaned into her face and whispered, "Will your God save you from *me*? Better yet, will he save you from this?"

Slice.

The left side of her cheek tore open from the scalpel just like a knife cutting through some soft, creamy butter.

"Aahh!" screamed the angel as she flailed her arms wildly to quickly get away from me. During this moment, I quickly noticed something fell out of a strange pocket that she had sewn into the right shoulder portion of her shirt.

It was an antique-style key, and it looked like my future just got a hell of a lot brighter. Snatching the key up before it even hit the ground, I ran toward the entrance door. Fear had my stomach almost literally tied in knots. Would the angel attack me from behind? Would she try to kill me, seeking some vigilante justice because I thoroughly enjoyed watching her priest die? So many things to ponder . . .

Fumbling with the key in the doorknob, I surprisingly found that it fit the keyhole perfectly. Several seconds later, I felt a hand on top of my left shoulder. Before I had a chance to react, the angel quickly grabbed me and threw me back into the room. The precious freedom I thought was mine was now actually gone forever in just a moment's notice. The key was now gone from my grasp, and with its loss, so too was any semblance of freedom from this freaking nightmare. Hell on earth . . . not even I could appreciate this strange moment in time. As she hurtled toward me with the tenacity of some less benign creature, her glowing white eyes seemed to almost burn with hatred for me. Without warning, her hands clenched tightly around my throat. As she squeezed with all her might, I could quickly feel my air passage-way tighten up. Even if I wanted to breath, there was no way of even fathoming the attempt from my air passage. As my breathing slowed to almost a complete halt, I began to succumb to an unconscious realm as I passed out on the cold concrete. Having her way again, I was still the angel's subject to torture, the very wicked being to cleanse or purge of all of my ways . . . whatever.

The next day.

When I woke up, my throat was sore, and it felt strange to swallow anything at all. Looking around me, I noticed that I had been placed back on the disgusting old mattress that had been laid out on the floor for me. Something strange had happened to my left hand. I tried to move it, but it was restrained somehow by . . . a metal clasp held tight against my wrist. Old and rusty, a metal chain was attached to it that led toward a metal pipe in the back of the room that held the other metal clasp to keep everything together. Staring at it, I could not believe my eyes. Everything was spiraling out of my control, and I couldn't do anything about it . . . not yet. Reluctantly, I regretted not killing off the angel when we had first encountered each other on the mountain. Was that evil to think? Dreaming of the torture that I could inflict upon an innocent angel? Her slain body just oozing out God's own precious blood that had previously given her life . . . just to have it snuffed out in a moment's notice.

Evil? That's my innate nature . . . primal. The kind of primal evil in nature that dates back to Adam and Eve, who in nature bit the apple . . . but who tempted Eve in nature to bite the apple? It was me . . . the coaxed, the instigator, and the overall filth that destroys all innocence. So . . . why couldn't I destroy the angel?

Chapter Thirteen

THE CHANGELING

Moments later, I began to try to free myself from the strange metal shackle that was attached to my left hand. Twisting and turning my wrist around, the only thing that actually occurred was one small trickle of blood that slowly ran down my arm and began to pool in the crook of my elbow. Curiosity taking over, I took my right pointer finger and scooped up some of my blood that had pooled in the crook of my arm. Smearing the blood on my lips, I instantly felt a burning sensation—almost as if my lips were about to catch on fire. Quickly, my tongue darted out to soak up the blood that was on my thin, pale lips, and the burning sensation was finally vanquished.

A moment of absolutely nothing passed me by . . . until it was my time.

The changeling.

Feeling slight nausea in the pit of my stomach, I felt something inside my body slightly shift, as if getting in position for an incident that was soon to occur within me. Suddenly, rolling waves of nausea completely took over my body, and I could not control the urge to vomit. I tried, but all my attempts failed, and nothing would produce out of my throat.

Without warning, my body broke apart into hundreds of different pieces, and I quickly morphed into several dozen ravens that immediately took flight out of an open window ten feet above the cold concrete floor. The locked door may have banned my freedom, but the open window above had just granted blessed freedom instead of my previous imprisonment . . . now I was truly airborne into my own sacred freedom.

With ebony, glossy wings flapping through the breeze, it seemed as if several hours had passed before I could reach my final destination. Believe it or not, my travel by flight landed me just above the train from which I had been kidnapped by the jaded angel. Seeing the broken ceiling glass where the bathroom had been, I made my entrance. By the time I had arrived in the bathroom, my morphing back into my human form was already near completion. Trying to act natural, I went back to my seat and instantly fell asleep. Funny thing though, the passage of time had not sped up or slowed down. Actually, it seemed as if time itself had stopped during my departure, only to be brought back to life again upon my entrance. Sounded great to me, I was in need of some much-needed rest after my ordeal with the angel.

The angel . . . what was her name? I hoped to never find out as long as my existence on this forsaken earth was still intact.

Drifting off on the wings of a deeper sleep than I had ever known before, I soon felt all of my pain slowly ebb away with every moment of sleep that carried me away into the night.

With heavy beams of light filtering in from the large window, I quickly awoke to the sound of slowing wheels on the train tracks and the sweet aroma of some much-needed coffee. Holding my hand up to wave over one of the assistants on the train, I politely asked for some coffee and a Danish. Famished, I wolfed down the food in nearly thirty seconds. Looks of disgust came from several of the passengers, but I didn't care. After everything that I had been through, they could stick it where the sun don't shine. My throat was still sore from when the angel had previously strangled me, so ingesting coffee was a bit cumbersome. After the train came to a complete halt, I stood up and quietly made my way toward the exit door of the train. As I stepped down and gingerly placed my foot onto the pavement, I noticed that it felt hotter outside than it had the past week. Maybe the rainy days of spring were just a thing of the past.

Anyway, I looked around and everything seemed normal, or so I thought at the moment. Scanning the area, I slowly noticed someone out of the left corner of my eye.

My blood ran *cold*, and I felt as if I could pass out on the scorching pavement at this exact instance. Approximately ten feet away, staring me dead in the face, was the angel that had previously kidnapped me. Still, an instant later, I blinked and she was gone.

Shrugging it off as a hallucination from the chaos I endured, I carried on with my great escape plan. Realizing that I had to strategize what to do next, I carefully sat down on one of the train station benches and thought of a plan. What should I do next? Would the angel eventually catch up to me? Or would I never see her again? Worry and self-doubt began to take control of my mind. Several moments later, I had finally thought up a plan to finish up my great escape. First, since it was still morning, I would hike the rest of the way toward the Austrian border. Not being able to afford any unwanted attention, I had to hastily make plans to quickly distract one of the attendants at the Austrian border crossing area. Maybe I could possibly coerce one of the people crossing over the Austrian border to distract the attendants while I quickly made my getaway from all of the chaos I would finally be leaving behind in my life.

It sounded good to me, so I carried on with my hike, the grass softly crunching beneath my feet. Secretly, I thanked myself that I had packed at least a month's worth of survival essentials . . . just in case of . . . tragedy.

Chapter Fourteen

BEST FRIENDS FOREVER . . .

Not that anything would ever happen to me, but I just liked knowing my plan of action ahead of time. Preparation for whatever lay ahead was better than anything else I could possibly come up with at the moment. Dredging on, I began my hike toward the Austrian border of my country. Not the nicest or safest way to travel, but it was at least better than being caught by the vicious police department in my country. Stopping for a quick lunch, I ate some trail mix and granola bars before carrying on to the designated area. After I was able to cross the border, I could call one of my friends who conveniently lived an hour away from . . . Damn, I better call her now!

Dialing her number, I captured my friend's voice on the second ring from my phone. Before I could say one word, my best friend, Agatha, sternly stated, "At the border, car running . . . just make it a mile down the hill." *Click*.

Realizing she knew that I was trying to make a great escape helped, since I had called her a week before I buried that insignificant and worthless excuse of a human, also referred to as my ex-boyfriend. Pushing those memories aside, I carried on with my mission. Still, having an hour before my destination, I truly knew that time was of the essence. Knowing this spurred me on to complete even one more goal I had lived up . . . killing my best friend.

In previous years, we had been the best of friends. Without warning, she decided to move to another country, for reasons unknown . . . other than the fact that she had slept with my ex-boyfriend recently. It was unknown to me, until I discovered something a bit odd in my laundry basket after she decided to flee to a different country . . . her underwear and bra! How did I know it was hers? Well, it wasn't mine . . . she fled a country to get away from my wrath . . . just put two and two together on this subject. I was not any part of that ensemble, I can prove that! Still, that was not the discovery that sealed tight my suspicions of cheating. My suspicions were actually confirmed when I checked my boyfriend's texts messages on his phone. Also, there were pictures . . . of her, of him, oh hell, and even one beautiful picture of them together in bed.

May they burn in the ninth circle of hell.

Did I seriously just contemplate that? Most definitely. I selfishly wished to be the great one at the judgment gates, just to watch them both end up burning in hell.

Hell hath no fury like a woman scorned. Feel my wrath you wretched idiot! Messing with me was like being the queen and on top of the ant hill . . . and I was the ultimate bully sadistically holding the magnifying glass to burn her alive.

Anyway, putting the incident aside, I carried on to my final destination. If I didn't push down my irrational thoughts about this whole ordeal, I might end up *really* mentally disturbed for the rest of my years on this unforsaken earth. Treading on, I finally sat down for a quick bite at the halfway mile marker. Quickly preparing my meal, I had a peanut butter and jelly sandwich and a side order of potato chips held in a small plastic bag. Hungrily munching away, I never realized until now how hungry I had actually become. Less than two minutes later, my meal was complete.

Quickly standing up, I knew not to waste any more precious time—it might mean a matter of life or death. If I actually survived this entire ordeal. Later on, I discovered that the border wall was only ten feet in front of me. Being in a completely open field with no trees or shrubbery to hide within, I quickly devised a plan.

First, I would lie down in the knee-high grass and crawl toward the exact spot I needed to arrive at next in my overall plan. Feeling foolish, my face red, I realized the Austrian border patrol was just over a mile away from me. Still, going undetected could not hurt my great escape plan overall.

Looking up, I noticed the ten-foot, concrete wall dauntingly above me. It almost felt like it was mocking me, saying, "Hey, fat chance you could ever climb over this wall . . . you might as well stop before you get ahead of yourself." Still, the border wall seemed extremely daunting until I noticed that it had many various crevices in it, as if it were sculpted more for rock climbing. With that concept in mind, I took off hiking at lightning speed, quickly resting on top of the border for only a mere second. Once, I cranked my neck to see if any of the guards bothered to notice me. To my initial shock, no one had noticed me. As I positioned my body to climb down the other side of the wall, I quickly looked over to where the Austrian border patrol agents were currently positioned. Without warning, one of the patrol men turned to look me dead in the eye. My blood ran *cold* as ice, even though beads of perspiration began to form along my forehead. What was I supposed to do now?

Frantically thinking of a way to escape the patrol men, I looked down from the top of the wall. Squeezing my eyes together tight, I let my hands go and fell down ten feet toward the ground below me. Landing on some thick underbrush lessened the fall a bit, but I still landed with a heavy thud and thought I heard something snap around my left ankle. Sure enough, I inspected my ankle and noticed that I had sprained it, to the point that there was no possible way of walking with my left foot. Nothing seemed to be actually broken internally. How would I get down the steep hill to meet my best friend waiting patiently in her car?

Roll over.

So, I got up and found enough energy to start at the top of the hill. Rolling down, I felt as if I was physically demonstrating how my life had quickly spun out of control. If people hadn't ultimately provided me with a burned me in my life, then I wouldn't have to kill them. Fair enough . . . right? I know!

"You reap what you sow . . ." A faint whisper reached my ears, but when I glanced around to look, there was absolutely nothing. Shrugging it off as a figment of my imagination, I finally completed my rolling down the gigantic hillside. Slowly standing up afterward, I noticed my best friend in her car, waiting for me. She seemed to be staring at me with an impatient look on her face as if to say, "Will you please hurry up! I have to get you back to my place, where you will actually end up in somewhat of a safe zone, for the time being."

Frantically playing with the car handle, she finally gave a huge shove, and it swung open to quickly allow me inside. Running toward her, I slid into the front passenger seat and slammed the door behind me. Blank stares with a monotone voice led to her present comment, "You're in trouble. How you got there, I have no idea, but I am here for whatever help you currently need."

Without warning, she slammed on the gas pedal, and I was thrown forward, since I had forgotten to wear my much-needed seat belt. Strapping down, I looked at her and said, with no sign of dread or fear in my voice, "Calm down. No one is even following me."

"Then who the hell is that man standing in the middle of the road?" my friend asked in confusion.

I looked in the rearview mirror. I could recognize that man anywhere. He was the Austrian border patrol guard who had previously witnessed me climbing to the other side of the border wall. Are you kidding me? How did he make it that far? Wasn't he a mile away?

"If we are lucky, he didn't write down my license plate number," said my friend with contempt in her voice. *Yeah, she should be the one with contempt after everything she put me through this past year,* I seriously thought to myself. Instead of shooting her a vicious look of contempt, I actually just put my head down and closed my eyes to take a minute for myself. I had been through a lot in the past week, and snapping at her would only make matters worse.

Especially since I wanted to get away with murdering my best friend . . . no questions asked!

Setting all emotions aside so I could maintain my cool would be an essential element to carrying through with my main objective . . . her lifeless body looking up at me in complete shock and horror. Breaking the ice, I said, "Want some?" I asked offering her a piece of gum.

"At a time like this? Oh well, you know me, I'm not really one for passing by anything or saying no," she said as she grabbed herself a piece of Big Red gum.

Among other things, you can't say no to my dead ex-boyfriend, I thought to myself. Wow, I really needed to work on my emotions if I was actually going to pull this off successfully. Driving on, my best friend, Agatha, continued for about a mile down the road until we finally arrived at our destination. She pulled into her winding driveway and put the car in the parked position. Before getting out of the car, she quickly asked, with legitimate concern strewn all over her face, "Are you going to be all right?"

"Yeah, as long as you're here to get me through this, I can emotionally make it," I said with a fake grin that I deceptively made look sincere.

"All right, let's quickly get inside—I heard the weather report today, and it might rain soon."

"Let's go," was the only response that I uttered back.

Quickly getting inside, I forgot how amazing her home was in contrast to mine. A spiral staircase going up three flights of stairs carried with it many hidden secrets between my dead ex-boyfriend and my best friend, Agatha. The walls were painted white to contrast the brown leather furniture. Off in the distance, a grand piano rested. The ivory whites of the various piano keys could have been witnessed a mile away, the contrast almost too vivid against the black lacquer paint. To say the interior of the house was amazing was completely an understatement. Walking over to the kitchen, Agatha the looked at me and asked, "Want something to eat?"

Famished from not eating any full meals on a consistent basis, I quickly followed her into the kitchen. Around fifteen minutes later, she had prepared two plates of chicken fettucine alfredo paired with two Bosco sticks filled with mozzarella cheese. Less than two minutes later, I had devoured my meal and went for the large glass of milk that patiently waited in anticipation in front of me.

Before I could completely grasp the full cup of milk, Agatha had taken it away from me. Puzzled for a second, I quickly wondered what was going on until she switched the drink to a cold draft beer instead.

"You've been through enough this past week, just like you said earlier, so you really deserve this." In agreement, I held the ice-cold beer to my pale, thin lips and drank half of it within a minute.

"Guess you needed it more than I thought," said Agatha with a smirk on her face.

"Guess so," I stated, and I took the rest of the cool liquid down my throat. After that, I told her that I was in need of some much-needed rest. Agreeing, she showed me the guest bedroom, and she walked directly across from it to sleep in her own bedroom. Drifting off to a deeper realm of slumber, I suddenly realized why I had a smirk on my face.

I imagined her own smirk on her face earlier as she gave me the beer replaced with a look of shocked anguish and pain as I plunged one of the kitchen knives deep into her chest.

Well, a girl could dream big if she wanted to after all . . .

The next morning, we both got dressed and prepared ourselves to go to the market for a few groceries—just the essentials, nothing too major. No filet mignon or porterhouse steak, that was for damn sure. Before we decided to leave, she quickly asked, "Are you sure you're not staying here instead? I am only getting a few items. What about that patrol man we saw yesterday? Stay safe and stay low for a few days."

"All right," I agreed, and I remained inside the house. While she was gone, I decided to look around each room to see what could possibly be used for weapons. Of course, there were the obvious knives in the kitchen. In the bathroom, I noticed the dental floss could possibly be used for strangulation if I planned it out ahead of time.

Tragedy.

Anyway, after a brief overview of the house, I decided to go outside, where there was a small garden. Snipping several roses off their stems, I made a great display of them in the center of her table. In the clear glass vase, the roses seemed to be almost floating in an ambient light as the sun reflected its various rays upon the water in the vase. After a few minutes, Agatha was back with the essentials she needed from the grocery store.

"Do you need any help with that?" I asked, pointing toward her grocery bags.

"No thank you, Desdemona, I can handle it," said Agatha, as she hurried into the kitchen. After a while, she brought back some champagne glasses with some sort of bubbly essence inside of them. On the left side of each was a succulent red strawberry.

"Wow, you bought us drinks? Oh, thank you, Agatha!" I exclaimed as she handed me my specified glass to sample it. Actually, it tasted like a mix between a juicy, delicious red apple and very tart and tangy lemon.

"Nice choice," I said.

"Thanks" was the only response that I received from Agatha. After we were finished, I politely left the room to go to the bathroom. Upon entering, I carefully took a peek through her medicine cabinet. There were bottles for melatonin, Zoloft, Adderall, and Tylenol. The one medication that truly caught my eye was the . If I overdosed her, without her realization, maybe that would be a more effective end to the life of a two-bit whore. Wait . . . did I say that? No, but I sure as hell was thinking it after what she did to me—or technical, what she and my ex-boyfriend had actually done together, without any of my knowledge. Maybe she would go out this way. Remembering what a bloody mess my ex-boyfriend's murder had been, I was glad I wasn't the cleanup crew for that mess.

Tragedy.

Chapter Fifteen

DISCOVERED ITEMS WRAPPED IN SINISTER INTENTIONS

You have to admit, hell hath no fury like a woman scorned. Hiding my emotions from Agatha would be tricky, but if I played my cards right, this would be one to play back on the tape recorder in my own twisted mind's memories.

Walking down the stairs, I noticed something odd from the corner of my peripheral vision—navy-emblazoned white lettering that said, "Some people have it, others don't . . ." I could have recognized that T-shirt anywhere. Actually, it was my dead ex-boyfriend's T-shirt that we had bought together on a shopping trip just before we had moved in together.

Holy shit.

Not only did my best friend deserve to die, but I was also elated due to the fact that my currently dead ex-boyfriend could never again place his grubby hands on any woman ever again. Setting emotions aside, I completed my walk down the stairs and into the kitchen. If she asked any questions, I would feel free to answer . . . yeah right! In the living room, Agatha turned on the television and quickly stated, "All right, I just put in a movie for both of us to watch. Are you ready?"

While I was gone, she had already prepared some home-made popcorn and root beer floats for the two of us . . . then

I vividly remembered my ex-boyfriend's T-shirt just innocently sitting on top of her bed. Innocently staring at me . . . judging me . . . mocking me with just the absolute fact that it was there and it existed, just a crude reminder from the past that burned me to the very core of any semblance of a soul I might actually still have residing within me.

"No!" I screamed out loud, surprising even myself with the irrational outburst. "What I meant to say was no, how about we just binge-watch some television show instead?" I asked my best friend.

"That's fine with me," Agatha stated plainly.

She allowed me to make the final decision as to what exactly we would be watching on the television.

My choice?

I chose a melodrama with a very significant title to coincide with the entire plotline that described in two words my ultimate future plans for Agatha.

Sweet Revenge.

What could be better than that? Hopefully, she wouldn't be clever enough to catch on to my not-so-timid innuendo about upcoming future events. Clearly, she didn't, since we watched the first few minutes in complete silence before she interjected, "Can't believe anyone could do that to another human being . . . just cheat with their friend's guy. That's unforgivable," said Agatha in a snotty manner.

Are you kidding me with this . . . seriously? There may have been no signs of physical pain, but emotionally I felt the absolute stinging pain of resentment. It felt like a heavy weight was placed on my chest and I couldn't breathe at all. Gaining back my composure, I said aloud, fondly looking at my friend with my huge black eyes, "Thank God for people like you to trust. You're the best friend ever, Agatha."

I wanted to give in to my temptations to literally throw projectile vomit all over my current comment.

Anyway . . .

"Thanks, Desdemona, you're not too bad yourself." She said this with a smirk on her face, but I quickly caught the underlying message that she was giving me.

Slap that stupid smirk she had appearing on her face ...

Make her pay for what she did ...

Bitter resentment.

Don't know what it means to feel pain, Agatha? Later, we will have a little arrangement about that matter. Dead and bloated, her dead carcass would just be pleading for the pain to stop, since there would be an entire continuation in the ninth circle of hell. Hell . . . that is where all the whores resided anyhow, so Agatha would have no problem fitting in that specified location.

Bitter resentment.

Sure, that was a little bit grotesque about what would happen to Agatha, but she deserved it! She was a compulsive liar, a fraud, and good-for-nothing, miscreant filth of a human being. So, in that respect, I had no choice but to eventually kill her.

How would I accomplish this task? I contemplated.

Even with the previous macabre thoughts that I previously had about Agatha's demise, I kept it completely calm and collected in front of her the entire time we were watching the show.

Chapter Sixteen

A NICE GAME OF VOLLEYBALL

Wow, I thought I even liked Agatha? *I am so full of shit right now*, I secretly thought to myself. After the movie, we both decided to go outside and play some volleyball in her back-yard. The weather may not have been picture-perfect, but you could wear a T-shirt and jeans with no jacket required. During the volleyball game, we played in complete silence before Agatha said, "I'm glad to finally have you arrive at my house. It seems like it's been forever since we have hung out together . . . it gets so lonely always being by myself."

Then she gave me that tell-all smirk, the one you know means she is hiding something that is beyond all relevance of anything portrayed as innocence. Noticing her manner, I realized she was great at portraying innocence. Still, she was never actually innocent during her "portrayal."

Her smirk almost seemed to be mocking me, as if to say, "Yeah, I have been lonely, minus all the times that I sadistically slept with your boyfriend behind your back."

Figures.

Now it was my turn to serve the volleyball over the net. I was so angry, I took that volleyball and smacked it over the net . . . and it landed dead center on Agatha's face!

"Sorry! Oh, I didn't mean to, Agatha. Are you all right? Do you need anything?" I asked, kneeling over her with legitimate concern strewn all over my countenance.

A moment of silence passed between both of us.

Suddenly, Agatha stammered between sobs, "Ye-yeah I ne-need some Kleenex pl-plea-please." Taking her hand away from her face, she quickly let loose a heavy, bloody stream that began right underneath her nostril and ended up steadily dripping down toward the center of her chin.

Running toward her house, I almost slammed into the kitchen countertop as I grabbed a roll of paper towels to stop Agatha's blood flow. Not to make her blood run cold, just to stop her from bleeding . . . for now. Sprinting with the paper towel toward Agatha, I broke a piece off and administered very basic first aid to her. After five minutes of consoling her and applying pressure to her nose, all of the bleeding subsided. The only remnants of blood were on the volleyball and her hands, which I quickly cleaned up as well, once she recovered.

"So sorry for that, Agatha. It was an honest accident," I said while helping her stand up.

"It's all right, Desdemona. I really wasn't paying attention," she said as she wrapped her arm over my shoulder and I slowly guided her back into her home. Weariness or slight fatigue from the blood loss was what I was monitoring now, but she seemed to have no symptoms at the moment.

How naïve you are, Agatha, I completely did that on purpose.

That smirk on her face . . .

Pushing all of my internal thoughts aside, I sat down on the couch and put on some television for us. Agatha, on the other hand, went into the bathroom to check out the level of damage that occurred to her nose.

Sadistically, I thought, *Your nose is damaged? Your true concept of knowing you're damaged is when your insides are on your outsides . . . then I really know you have guts! You know, instead of being some gutless whore who has slept with my boyfriend, multiple times, and deserves to rot in hell!*

Suddenly, I could see Agatha walking down the stairs from the corner of my eye.

Anyway . . .

Back to my present life, back to my present reality . . . which currently sucked.

"Oh, Agatha, how do you feel?" I asked with legitimate concern.

Totally faking it right now, I was acting so fake toward Agatha, I might have well been some form of AI, a robot just performing the mere tasks of human communication but lacking all the feelings and emotions that made humans such truly complicated beings.

"Well, I feel better since the bleeding has stopped. Hey, accidents happen, right?" said Agatha, with her hands held up and a cute expression on her face.

I hated her with every core fiber of my being. Quickly hiding that fact, I said

"That's right, Agatha, and again, I do apologize for everything . . ."

"It's fine, Desdemona. I'm not really big on any sports or outdoor activities like that, so it was bound to happen." She grinned broadly at me while she squeezed my right shoulder in passing.

Finally, we sat down, and we watched several movies together until we both fell asleep on the couch. Sadly for Agatha, this would be the last peaceful sleep she would have tonight, as the preclude to her eternal restful sleep that I would enforce on her poor soul . . . the very next glorious day.

Chapter Seventeen

CRUEL INTENTIONS

The next day, I woke up, startled not to find another person in the room. Where was Agatha? Searching throughout the entire house, I finally found Agatha where she originally belonged—in her bedroom, with her mouth hanging open and drooling profusely . . . figures. Slowly walking away, I almost felt bad for Agatha, even if it was only slightly.

Looking down on the floor, I noticed a hat that my ex-boyfriend used to always wear during the summer months. Lying on the floor, with its black canvas colored with silver trim on the brim, it called to me.

"Hey, guess why I'm here! I should have slept with her right in front of your stupid face! Ha-ha-ha!"

Quickly, I hurried out of the bedroom and almost ran down the stairs to avoid the taunting and abusive rants of the hat that flew into the imagination of what my mind had recently created.

My face crimson red, I could not believe what had just happened. Not one but two of my ex-boyfriend's items had been lying on my best friend's bedroom floor. So much for best friends, that door had been shut a long time ago, only due to several "incidents" that quickly led me to the suspicion that my boyfriend had cheated on me multiple times with my now soon-to-be-dead, ex-friend Agatha.

Living in a completely different, strange realm of reality, I felt an ominous entity slowly take over my entire body. I felt an internal darker presence that resided within the very depths of my soul. My feelings were completely full of hate. Red-hot, seething rage toward Agatha began to grow within me, until I could not contain myself any longer. Without hesitation, I quickly grabbed the kitchen knife from the kitchen knife display that was placed conveniently in the center of the kitchen island.

As I ran up the stairs, the kitchen knife was still tightly gripped in my pale and trembling left hand.

Closing in on her bedroom door, I waited a moment in silence, calming my breathing down so that my heart rate from the anticipation would not give me away—the anticipation for what lay before me just being quickly put out of its misery.

Carefully, I slowly opened the door to her bedroom, with just enough space to allow my body to slide into the room. Snoring heavily, Agatha was in a deeper realm of sleep than what I had previously anticipated. Making my first move, I leaped on top of her while simultaneously covering her mouth with my right hand.

The first slash hit her throat, but no arteries were severed at the moment. Trying to let out her screams of anguish, Agatha was now obviously fully awake. Her eyes were bulging out in sheer terror at the sight of me on top of her while wielding the now crimson-red kitchen knife.

Writhing and flailing her arms, I knew that she was not going down without a fight. Thinking fast, I put the full weight of my right knee on top of her throat to commence slight suffocation. She tried to grab the knife away from my hand, but I viciously slapped her across the face. In retaliation, she bit my left hand so hard that it began to bleed. Teeth marks could be obviously seen on my hand too.

I cried out in agonizing pain at the sudden realization of her viciously drawing blood from her biting me. Well, my retaliation was much swifter. As I eased up my right knee that had been placed on top of her throat, I replaced it with a vicious, deep throat slash that hit her main artery.

Tragedy.

Splashes of warm blood sprayed across my face, and as her breathing slowed down to a halt, I knew that her demise was my ultimate victory. Time was now of the essence, but my ultimate victory had finally come to pass in what seemed like just a fleeting moment in time.

Splashes of warm blood were splattered across my face, and as her breathing slowed down to a final halt, I knew that her demise was my own personal victory. It had finally come to pass; the world was now rid of Agatha now and forever. Immediately sliding away from her, I noticed all of the large amounts of blood that had pooled around her throat and upper torso. The sheets were all in disarray, with thick pools of blood starting to clot and stain around where her throat had been slashed.

Calmly walking into the bathroom, I stuck my hands out to turn the water on in the sink. As I rinsed my face off, the remnants of her blood slowly drained away in the sink, never to be seen again. Still, all of that blood in her bed was going to be a serious problem.

Walking back into the bedroom, I luckily found some clean bedding sheets in her laundry basket. Wrapping her up in them, with her body on the floor, I secured them enough to drag her down into the basement. Dragging her down was not an easy task, especially when the stairs were involved. Several minutes would pass before you could hear a thud-thud-thud as her head hit against each individual stair going all the way toward the last bottom step. Frustrated by this, I quickly dragged her the rest of the way into the basement. Grimacing as I placed her body on the cold cement floor, I noticed my hands. Dark pools of crimson-red blood completely covered both my hands. Sadistically, I wrote one message in blood against the wall directly above her: Tragedy.

I regretted nothing as I calmly walked up the stairs. The door was still cracked open. Sliding past so that I didn't leave any blood on the door, I still noticed a bloodstained smear on the door handle.

Carefully, I washed my hands in the kitchen sink and then took bleach and paper towels to the door handle to clean up the blood smears. Shutting the door behind me, I noticed that there was a small hole underneath the door handle, to insert a small key to lock the door in place. Well, if I could find that key, it might spare me some time with the authorities. Great, now I had to contemplate another great escape plan.

Figures.

A moment of silence passed while I contemplated the next step that I would make in my plan.

Chapter Eighteen

SURPRISING INTRUDER

Suddenly, I heard a slight creak of the basement door, and I whirled around to inspect what was occurring during that moment. Oddly, the basement door that had been previously shut was now slightly open.

"I know that I had just shut the basement door," I quietly said to myself. As I walked closer to it, the basement door swung wide open and hit me dead center in the face. Reeling back from the pain, I held both my hands up to cover my face. Between my fingers I could see a figure in front of me.

The angel that previously kidnapped me was now back for some sweet revenge. I was not sure if she was mentally sending me messages, but one word entered into my mind: Lillith.

Appearing pissed off—well, as much as an angel could be— she seemed a lot taller than previously . . . and meaner.

Shock and dismay plagued my face before I asked, "Is your name Lillith?"

"Yes," she coolly stated.

"Did you telepathically send your name to me?" I asked.

"Yes," she uttered calmly.

My blood ran ice-cold at the mere thought of that concept. Lillith took one step closer to me. Angrily poking me in the chest she said, "It's like you're trying to take a tape recorder and fast-forward another person's death. You're not the grim reaper you're not the introduction to death. That's why he is angry with you, Desdemona. You can't cheat death just by finding justice in causing death to other people . . . it's simply not part of our rule book. We have rules here . . . remember the proper balance that controls everyone. Heaven and hell, the Almighty God and the devil himself." From her white, silken cloak, she pulled out the rule book. "Centuries ago, God and the devil made a pact to make this rule book to set aside their differences about who should actually inherit the earth. Without the rule book, there would be no balance. Chaos would ensue, and the world would not like the end result."

Bewildered, I looked at her with a brand-new sort of respect.

Dream on.

If I ever had any respect for her, I could never be the person, or demon, that currently inhabited me, which made me who I was today.

"If this rule book is centuries old, then why have I never heard of it?"

"There was a more popular book that took its place."

"What?"

"The Bible."

"What about the Book of Shadows . . ."

"Desdemona, stop being ridiculous!"

Grimacing at the mere thought of it, I turned to walk away from Lillith. Grasping my shoulder with a firm grip, she spun me around to face her. Drawing near, she whispered, "You can't cheat death yourself . . . all of your misdeeds will soon catch up to you."

Lillith's all-white eyes were glowing and seemed to be full to the brim of hatred, instead of some divine light from the heavens above this unforsaken earth.

Without thinking clearly, I made a mad dash for the upstairs room. For some stupid reason, I ran into the same room in which I had previously murdered my best friend, Agatha.

A moment of silence passed throughout the entire house.

Thud-thud-thud was all that I could hear echoing through the halls as Lillith slowly made her way up the stairs.

For several minutes, nothing happened, and everything remained silent. Until . . . viciously swinging the door open, Lillith quickly looked around the room and was livid.

With huge amounts of blood everywhere, the scene was not really registering as "innocent" to this self-righteous, moralistic entity for the Almighty God himself. Lust-filled rage entered Lillith as she slowly approached me. With each tentative step, her white, glowing eyes grew more vicious, second by the second. The glow from her eyes was so intense that I had to shield my own eyes from being burned by those enraged orifices. If my days were numbered, this was it . . . no more hatred, no more insanity . . . just get it over with . . . yet when I brought my arm down to witness Lillith, she was gone without a trace.

Beside the sink, on top of the bloody knife, stood a mourning dove. It screeched at me in one instant, an almost deafening sound that nearly broke my hearing all together. In one instant it was there, then it was gone in without a trace in the next instant.

Weird shit.

Thinking back, everything that I had accomplished up to this point had some valid motivation. Are you kidding me? I was the bad person in this situation? Someone had to be joking with me, but at the current time, hell, my entire life just seemed like one big joke.

Was it? What was the purpose to my life?

Kill or be killed was always my motto. I guess people had to learn the hard way about how *not* to mess with me at all. Contemplating messes, I quickly realized how much I needed to escape Agatha's house *now* before it was too late. Quickly running down the stairs, I grabbed the car keys that were lying on the kitchen countertop. Making a mad dash toward the entrance door, I quickly made my exit out of Agatha's house. Noticing her car was still fortunately in the driveway, my purest intention was currently stealing my best friend's car that was patiently waiting for me. Taking it all, since she had taken my ex-boy-friend enough times, seemed justifiable.

Statistics say that a brand-new auto theft claim is created every six minutes in my country. Well, right now there was another auto theft about to happen . . . all thanks to me.

Chapter Nineteen

MY GREAT ESCAPE PLAN

Hopping into the car, I hurriedly stuck the key in the ignition and started up the vehicle. Mere seconds later, I was hauling out of her driveway in reverse and turning into the street before me. In about zero to sixty seconds, my speed went up to an amazing eighty miles per hour. Thinking back to the border patrol man and police in general, I noticed the speedometer and brought it back down to a more proper speed of about forty miles per hour. Getting noticed by authorities now, in a stolen vehicle, was not anything that I could afford at this time.

Driving about twenty miles away from her house finally brought me to my destination. In a back alleyway, I decided to ditch the stolen car and throw the rear license plate in the bottom of a nearby dumpster. Using the disgusting trash that already resided in the dumpster, I quickly covered up the license plate so that it was completely out of sight. Suddenly, I thought of a much better plan. I dug through the remains in the dumpster and retrieved the license plate from the dumpster. In a rush, I placed the plate in my backpack, which was for the hike that I would attempt to make soon. Luckily, it had been accidentally left behind in the passenger's seat of Agatha's car. Now rather than later, I knew that I had to escape, since time was of the essence.

Approximately two miles away was a river, and for now, that seemed to be a decent escape plan. So, quickly ditching the stolen car, I hurriedly made my way out of the back alleyway and headed toward a quieter and more secluded area. After an hour, I noticed that I had been shrouded away from being seen in plain sight. The densely created forest was just the area that I was destined to acquire for my ultimate protection. Finally, I gingerly walked toward the edge of the river. Setting my backpack down, I took out the plate number, swiftly swung my arm back, and let loose the license plate, which ended up drifting down the quickly moving current. There, try to find *that* you bona fide incompetent Bundespolizei.

Creating a small camp setup would be necessary for my survival overnight in the forest. First, I picked up various twigs and branches for some kindling to create a fire from scratch before dusk turned into the pitch-black unknown . . . nightfall. After that, I had to reach into my backpack again and grab the sealed-up, incredibly small tent for a safer night's overall rest. With everything set up, I decided to forego eating anything and instead fell fast asleep in my tent.

Mere seconds later, my body's physical retaliation to stay fully awake was set off by the attacks of anxiety, stress, and an overall need for all of my troubles to finally arrive to some means of an end. The day of reckoning for my past misdeeds would soon be upon me, now I had to realize when that actual time would be occurring. Drifting off into a deeper sleep than I had ever known before, my nightmares would soon become a reality that would haunt not only my mind but the very essence of my soul. Later that night, I was awoken by the heavy sound of rain falling down onto my weakly established pop-up tent. As I rose, a bolt of lightning struck the sky so fiercely that its very presence immediately lit up the sky for a mere moment in time. My heart began to race as I cautiously opened the tent entrance to reveal . . . absolutely nothing. Cool, black ink seemed to encompass everything surrounding me, to the point that I could barely see my own hand in from of my face. Looking up toward the heavens—which was not something I had any kind emotions toward—I noticed the full moon illuminating the eerie, black-ink colored sky that seemed to almost hold an ominous tone, as if it was trying to tell me something that was just barely held away from my grasp of it.

Suddenly, a heavy bolt of lightning crashed upon the midnight sky. It illuminated a strange entity flying near the top of the full moon. It felt menacing, something that I should now be avoiding entirely with haste. Before I could respond, the strange entity changed its flight pattern and began flying straight toward me, with its eyes fixated solely on me. Was its intent to kill me? Was I purposely being sought after for . . . well, many reasons come to mind why I would be, but I didn't believe that I deserved to die over my many indiscretions that I had committed.

Those huge, glowing white eyes seemed to bore into the very essence of my deepest desires. She knew that I wanted to kill her, and she was sure not going down without a meaningful fight. My hollowed-out, soulless cadaver encompassed what I truly was inside . . . dead. The angel flying straight toward me . . . wait . . . it was the same angel that kidnapped me from the train earlier.

Holy shit.

Chapter Twenty

DEMONIC DEMON VERSUS HEAVEN'S DIVINE

In the past, the only enemies I had to deal with were my boyfriend and later Agatha—from whom I hid my hatred for until the most opportune timing—but they were flesh-and-blood humans. This creature was nothing at all like anything that I had encountered in my entire existence on this forsaken earth. Before I could respond, she was now only a mere ten feet away from me and still flying at full tilt straight toward me. I took the toughest stance that I could possibly muster and braced myself for impact.

On the outside, my face was like a placid lake, but on the inside, the turmoil inside me was more like a tsunami. The turmoil inside only warned me to prepare for the worst-case scenario . . . whatever that may be. I was completely unsure at the moment. She was even closer now, and I braced myself with my arms crossed in front of me in a very defensive posture. Headstrong, I was willing to take this angel on for my own brand of justice . . . her death as my purest joy imaginable. Two feet . . . now one . . . the angel slammed into me with the full force of a heavy freight train, while I was just the mere tracks that she steadily ran over along the way to her greater destination.

I knew that her intent was to kill me, but there was no way in hell that I was going down without a fight. This was one battle that I did not intend on losing, so she better bring her A game to the battleground or feel the wrath of the devil himself.

After sliding on the ground for a good ten feet, it left some ill-intended skiff marks all the way from the bottom of my neck to the bottom portion of my lower back. On top of me now, she menacingly whispered in my ear, "If you think that for one second you can get away with murder, then you have it all wrong, Desdemona. Ever heard of the phrase, *Thou shall not kill?*"

"Ever heard of hypocrisy?" I quickly retorted. "It seems to me that your Almighty God would not give you any semblance of recognition if he knew you wanted to torture me when you kidnapped me off of a moving train . . . you . . .psycho!"

Enraged, I gave a heavy shove toward the angel to get her away from me. She landed in some weird mound of dirt, which ended up not even making her dirty at all. Figures. Getting up, she quickly pointed to the mound of dirt and stated, "Do you know who resides down in the depths of this mound of dirt, Desdemona? Well, it just so happens to be . . ." Then she flew up into the top portion of the tree she had previously fallen under, as if she were hiding from something. But what the hell did an angel have to fear?

Slowly, the huge mound of dirt began to slightly slide away to reveal a pale countenance slowly rising from its previous dirt nap.

Sheer terror took over my five senses as I quickly realized that it was tragically my ex-boyfriend back from the dead.

Necromancy . . . revenge at its finest . . .

"Wherever you may roam, I will follow you, Desdemona . . ."

My throat viciously tightened, making it impossible to even utter any sound. As he slowly stood up to face me after digging himself out of his dirt nap, I realized what truly scared me about him. It wasn't his countenance that scared me at all . . . it was his slashed throat. Various lengths of ragged pieces of skin hung loosely around his severely sliced neck. To describe his condition anymore would be too horrific, even for a woman like me.

"My throat hurts . . ." said my dead ex-boyfriend in an extremely harsh and raspy voice.

The utterance of vile comments exited my thin, pale lips before I had the chance to take my own words back. "I am glad you had your throat sliced up. It looks better that way . . . if only your insignificant throat could be silenced, then I wouldn't have to worry about anything." I pointed toward his rotting corpse. "Since your remains don't mean anything to me at all!"

Filled with rage at what I had previously done to him, he leapt at me in an attempt to strangle the very essence out of my tragic existence. Yet, as soon as he got a grip around my throat, he was gone without a trace in the very next instant.

"W-what? Where did he vanish to?" I turned around in a mixture of confusion and amazement, just to make sure that he was nowhere behind me. A sneak attack from him was the last damn thing that I needed in my life at the moment.

Laughter erupted from high above the treetop. I had completely forgotten that the angel had witnessed everything that had happened. Jumping down from the top of the tree, she flapped her wings a bit to allow a perfect landing on the ground when her feet finally made contact with the dirt.

"Was it all imagined? Did your ritual of necromancy prove to be nothing more than just smoke and mirrors?" Then, I thought for a moment. "Did you seriously use your powers to make me hallucinate *all* of that?" I asked her incredulously.

A small smirk slowly played on her thick lips as she uttered the obvious words that I completely dreaded hearing. "Yes, you are correct."

Lunging at her with a fury that surprised even myself, I slammed the angel against the tree that she had so freely been hiding in for the past few minutes. Pieces of tree bark and dirt dispersed themselves everywhere as Lillith the angel made solid impact with the tree. Leaning in closer to her, I slapped the angel across the face so hard that it almost made her head spin.

"Don't you *ever* use your powers against me like that again!" I bellowed in an unusual voice that was definitely not my own.

You know what Lillith did in response? She laughed at me! I was beginning to question if she still was on the right-hand side of God after all we had been through together. Infuriated by her incessant laughter, I wrapped my hands around her throat and attempted to choke the life out of the angel. Her response? Flinging me off of her as if I was some mere rag doll. I actually landed right beside the river, my hair actually floating at the very edge of it.

She was stronger than I had anticipated, and the fall had really knocked the wind out of me. Not being able to get up was going to be a serious problem, especially where I was currently located. Before I could respond, Lillith quickly looked at me in my current condition. Knowing that I was temporarily immobilized, she calmly walked over to me with such a cold look of contempt candidly placed on her countenance. Fearing nothing, I braced myself for her return while faking some semblance of unconsciousness so that she would be unaware of my next plan of attack. Would I make it out of this fight alive? Maybe. Was I truly willing to be murdered by an angel? Not a snowball's chance in hell.

As I was still unable to move, the angel quickly grabbed me by the hair and lifted me off the ground by a few feet. Kicking and screaming, I raked my left hand across her face, probably leaving a permanent scar underneath her right eye socket. Instinctively, she dropped me, and I fell into the river on the shallow end. She quickly wiped the smudge of blood from her cheek, and I felt a heavy thud against the back of my neck. She had her hand gripped around the back of my throat, and she was literally trying to drown me.

Something strange was at the left side of my face in the water with me. Thin and elegantly designed brown fingers crossed my eyesight as she snapped her fingers in the water. A moment of silence passed, minus my deliberate biting of her "sacred" hand in that water . . . while her other one was trying to murder me. Before I knew it, a slick, white animal was in the water swimming toward me. To my disgust, I noticed it was a white, venomous water snake, one of the deadliest varieties . . . did she call upon it with her powers? These snakes were not known for being in my country at all. It seemed to flow with the river, almost mesmerizing in its beautiful yet deadly overall essence. Unable to move, with the angel holding me down with the force of some press machine in operation, I began to panic. Then, the unthinkable happened.

It bit me . . . my tragedy.

They say that talking to angels can bring peace within a person . . . did anyone ever meet the wolf in sheep's clothing that I had to contend with? Finally, the angel known as Lillith ceased her grip around my neck, and I flung my head back quickly out of the water. Fresh air quickly entered my lungs as I took my first few inhaled breaths of freedom without the angel's grip on the back of my neck. I turned around to actually hit her, but she was already a foot back from the river, with the venomous white snake wrapped around her slender neck.

Was it the snake of virtue and truth, while I was only full of lies and deceit?

"May the almighty hand of God take pity on you, wretched woman!"

Livid with seething, hot rage toward Lillith, I slowly stood up and made my way toward her. Inches away from her perfect countenance, I viciously spat saliva right into her godly, self-righteous, and indignant face. I whispered, "I outshine you in ways you could never even comprehend, angel. My powers may not have come to me as a child, only after being abused as a full-fledged adult, you piece of . . ."

My throat viciously tightened, and I gripped my hands to my throat. Poison from the water snake was currently working its way into my system, restricting my breathing . . . until I was only barely alive.

My heart rate began to slow down . . . right before I punched the angel in the left eye socket. Hell, I was literally dying in front of her, and I needed her to have a permanent reminder of me . . . forever. So, I missed her eye and actually ended up breaking the left side of her jaw. What a sweet little victory . . . and then something suddenly struck me.

Tragedy.

Falling to the ground, I had many convulsions, eerily similar to an episode of an epileptic seizure. Burning sensations flew into my blood stream, and it felt as if someone lit a match and set my blood on fire inside of my body. Then, when the pain subsided, so did my existence on this forsaken earth. This was the day I literally died, and at least I knew deep down in my heart that my death was not to be taken in vain. I had taken the lives of others, of course, but I didn't regret a second of my epic endeavor.

Hungrily watching her blood spill on the floor of the riverbed, the angel silently watched Desdemona slowly waste away into nothingness.

She quietly thought to herself, *Was she nothing? Or was she worth something?*

She contemplated what she got on Desdemona, killer of two humans and a priest. *She got off lucky*, the angel thought to herself.

Flying in the sky, she noticed a mourning dove with a scroll clutched in one of its small talons. As she held her hand open, the dove flew low and gingerly dropped the elusive message into the palm of her hand. Without haste, she opened up the message, and her heart skipped a beat . . . out of complete fear.

Chapter Twenty-One

AN ANGRY MESSAGE
FROM HEAVEN

The message read: "Do you have any semblance of a conscious? In the world I know exists, my angels are not the ones doing the killing . . . ever heard of my historical phrase, *Thou shalt not kill?* Yours truly, the Alpha and the Omega . . . God."

Lillith's blood ran *cold* with the anticipation of her confrontation with the Almighty God. Included in the message was not a date and time to meet with him but an actual instruction to stop everything she was doing and meet him at once.

Without hesitation, she flew up into the heavens and left the now dead and bloated body of Desdemona far behind on the forsaken earth, where she never truly had a concrete home . . . neither did her now defeated enemy.

As she flew closer to her destination, Lillith's anxiety quickly took over her entire demeanor. This was not some royal nothing snob that she was about to encounter. It was the Almighty, the Alpha and the Omega, the Holy Messiah, and she slowly just came to the realization that she had completely pissed him off . . . royally.

Flowing, warm breezes could be felt against her cool skin right before she landed on heavens ground, directly in front of the Almighty God himself. What an awful confession she would have to make in front of such an amazing God. Would she be reprimanded? Only time would tell . . .

Finally, God began to speak, in a voice that sounded stern yet full of compassion for this specific angel all at the same time.

"What you are is an abomination to the exact benign and moralistic culture that I so meticulously crafted, eons ago," he bellowed in a voice that was far from angelic.

In absolute fear, Lillith took her translucent wings to completely cover her entire body for some semblance of protection. Feeling so cold all of a sudden, she began to slightly tremble in front of the Almighty God. To suffer the wrath of God was not something that should be taken lightly at all.

"I should place you in a rusty cage and let you *rot* for what you did to Desdemona. Yet, should I perform such acts of contrition? Soon, we shall see, my angelic Lillith—*not* so angelic after all, my dear."

A fearful moment of silence passed between the two entities that resided in heaven. Lillith's mind must have been sent into warp speed, thinking about what his end result would be for this now seemingly angelic woman who had a glimmer of a sadist residing within her. Wondering what God hated the most? Arrogance!

"You are the unforgiven angelic presence, which actual resides as something else . . . something much more sinister, Lillith." The way that he had said her name, with such contempt in his voice, was not a good sign. Suddenly, he beckoned the angel with his finger to quietly step closer toward him.

"Turn around, my dear. This may hurt a little," bellowed the Almighty with the utmost sternness in his voice. Slowly turning, Lillith was dreading every second of her encounter with the Almighty. For a moment, absolutely nothing happened. An odd pull began at the base of both of her wings, and then the tearing commenced . . . all of those beautiful feathers, thousands in all, plucked out to zero, which was incredibly painful for the angel to endure. Finally, with a tight grip on both of her wings, God ripped the angelic wings spread out for forgiveness of her lord . . . only to receive absolute pain for what she did to Desdemona in return.

Blue and black contusions began to form along the sides of where the base of her wings used to be, and now there was nothing residing there but blood and shame.

"Thou shalt not kill! I cast aside your angelic powers. You now live as a mere human . . . one whom most people will not look favorably upon . . . trust me!"

With that said, the Almighty gave a gigantic shove that sent Lillith falling straight down from heaven. She was an angel now begrudgingly falling from the heavens, only to reside for quite some time on that forsaken earth that she so despised.

What the Almighty didn't realize was that at that epic moment in time, he had created an absolute monster.

Chapter Twenty-Two

Still falling from the heavens above, Lillith only had one word burning into her memory. *Why?* Why had his punishment been so swift and painful? Why had his punishment almost seemed full of hate? Many questions swam together in her mind until that fateful moment. Lillith had hit rock bottom, and the meaning was literal. Crashing into various rocks and twigs, she shamefully had finalized her actual placement in heaven . . . non-existent. As heaven's gate literally closed behind her, she wept bitter tears of remorse. Moments later, due to her emotions, it began to rain, but only because the Almighty was weeping for her, for his loss that he had just had over this specific angel.

A moment of silence passed before she did anything. At least, surprisingly, God had been benign enough to make a soft landing for her, as a huge bed of grass and a slower pace of the fall before landing had helped her out tremendously. Now human, she shamefully stood up and checked out her surroundings.

Looking up, she noticed that there was a slight breeze that ran through the tops of the emerald-green tress that surrounded her in the forest. Off in the distance, she noticed a mourning dove flying in the sky, just another form of symbolism that her peaceful life in heaven had ended . . . but what would be her life on this forsaken earth? Far from heaven, that was the true realism of it. At the forest floor, she noticed a small, baby deer that was getting up on its legs after a restful nap. Another symbolism of innocence lost and how currently alone in the world she felt at that exact moment. Carefully walking forward, she walked for about a decent mile before she reached an open field, where a city could be seen within about five to six miles, if she did not stop her walk toward the unknown city. A recluse for so many years, she actually despised the idea of cities and preferred to live alone. Just another reminder she was truly going to be taught a lesson by the Almighty. As the ground squished underneath her feet after the recent rainstorm, she also noticed that the season here on earth was now summer. A slight breeze caressed her face as she journeyed on, an unknown entity in a very unknown setting on this forsaken earth.

About an hour into her journey, she finally arrived at the city. Looking around her, she felt an overwhelming sense of hope at the prospect of all the people surrounding her. Maybe some could even be saved by the Almighty . . . or was she still benevolent after what he had done to one of his most loyal angels? Smells of car exhaust and various foods lingered in the air as the many passersby were on their way to their own individual journeys. She saw a small child walking with his mother, and he made eye contact with Lillith and actually smiled, a response by actual humans she had almost forgotten. Now that she was one herself, she felt very humbled and considered the fact that instead of having a hand to guide her along the way, she was feeling even more alone in the bustling metropolis with all its congestion and her feelings of abandonment by her God. Surrounded by many people, she never felt more alone than at that moment.

The realization that she currently had no monetary funds nor a shelter to call her own left her feeling almost panicked, and quickly she began to try to find some sort of solution. Looking around, she noticed an older gentleman with a broom, sweeping the floors inside his bakery. The entrance door had been held wide open to allow all of the dust and debris out into the smog-riddled air outside.

Reluctantly walking into the shop, her bad timing ended with all of the dust and debris flying straight toward her face, like some sort of miniature dust storm that you would see out west.

"Oh, I am *so* sorry for that!" exclaimed the gentleman.

"That's fine, I am all right." She mustered up enough courage to shake his hand through irritated, watery eyes.

"I was wondering if you were hiring any type of help for your shop?" she asked through slightly clenched teeth. Also, the dust and debris had partially been ingested into her mouth, due to the unexpected occurrence.

"Actually, I am the owner of the shop. My most recent hire quit about a week ago, after *only* working for my business for a solid week . . . teenagers." He quietly snorted underneath his breath and went back to sweeping his floor.

"So, if there is an open position . . ."

With his back turned to me, while sweeping, he muttered, "You can start tomorrow morning at nine. Hopefully, you last longer than the others."

"Oh, thank you, sir, I really appreciate this . . ."

"Just show up on time, and you will do fine," he said, waving me back as several customers excitedly walked in to place their orders.

Maybe this being a human thing isn't so bad after all, the angel quietly thought to herself as she grabbed a raspberry scone and walked out of the bakery. Scanning the area, she noticed a cathedral off in the distance. With its freshly painted white-and-black trim, the overall fresh appearance made it seem that more benign. Unfortunately, it looked as if it were the only thing that had recently been updated in the past ten years, given the looks of what surrounded it.

Walking over, she followed the crosswalk signs exactly and excitedly made her way over to the cathedral. Never one for passing by a church, her instincts led her to believe that this would be the absolute haven that she could call home . . . for the time being. Approaching the black-ink doorknob, she opened her hand toward it and firmly gripped the knob before she realized . . . tragedy.

Searing heat began at the center of her palm and then spread out, as if trying to burn her out and away from the church altogether. Agonizing pain ensued, as the heat emanating from the doorknob was almost too much for her to handle. Trying to break free of its grip, she realized to her horror that she was not able to move her hand off the doorknob. Before she passed out from the pain altogether, whatever force was holding her hand there abruptly released her hand, for the rude awakening that she was about to witness next . . .

Looking down at the center of her palm, she noticed in finely written, small letters the actual statement that sank her heart deep inside her chest: "Thou shalt not kill."

It'd been carved into her flesh by the Almighty God himself, and she knew instinctively that her days on this earth were numbered. Her hand still trembling from the ramifications of that quote, she slowly walked toward the top of the stairs and sat down in an extremely defeated position. Hanging her head low, she slowly began to cry tears of resentment, bitterness, and absolute loneliness in this forsaken earth. As her tears turned into even bigger heaving sobs, a miracle happened . . . it began to rain.

Or was that just the Almighty God actually weeping for one of his dearly departed angels who would be absolutely lost to him for all eternity? Deep down, no one would ever really know, not truly.

After opening the door slightly, a tall, benign entity quickly walked over to the angel and knelt down beside her for slight consolation.

"Noticed you were out here all by yourself in the rain . . . mind stepping inside for a bit?" he said, as she slowly turned her head to look toward him.

Extremely younger than anticipated, the tall priest seemed to be about in his mid to late thirties, with black hair and hazel eyes deeply set in his countenance. Not moving, he patiently motioned for her to enter the cathedral. With the door still slightly open, it seemed as if the place was now changing its mind after all, allowing her inside its benign domain.

Slowly standing up, she made her way over toward the main entrance. Upon entering, she noticed the high arches and the attention to detail of the stained-glass windows at the sides of the room. One such window in particular immediately caught her attention. It was a stained-glass image of the Almighty God, upon resurrection at last. Still, there was something strange about the stained-glass image on the window. The entity seemed to be not only staring at her but actually *through* her, into the innermost reaches of her soul . . . or whatever semblance of soul that was leftover due to recent tragic events.

As the priest led her away from the room, he took her toward an actual bathroom in the back, where she could freshen up and later tell him of her current living situation—or lack thereof. Staring at her most recent flesh wound that had mysteriously appeared on her hand, she felt the shame of those words now more than ever.

"Thou shalt not kill."

Touching the wound, even with soap and water, she winced in pain at the sudden realization that there would always be a constant reminder of the one indiscretion she completed that would haunt her dreams for all eternity.

Stepping out of the bathroom, she noticed the priest was patiently waiting for her return. Before she could even utter one word, he quickly said, "If you are in need of some respite and a safe place to stay for a few days, you may stay here for the time being." Instinctively, without even thinking, she hugged the priest and muttered a thank-you for allowing her safety in the cathedral.

Walking her toward the kitchen area, he motioned with his hands for her to sit down at the table. Displayed in from of her were various meats, cheeses, and even wine. Her eyes bulged at the entire spread of the various foods before her.

"Are you sure about this?" the angel asked incredulously.

"Absolutely," said the priest, with a smirk on his face.

Famished, she ate nearly everything that was in sight, which was actually enough for a family of four. Face red with embarrassment, the priest quietly asked, "Are you homeless, without any means of an income?"

"Homeless, yes. But I just received a job today. I begin at 9:00 a.m. tomorrow."

"I will figure out some type of new clothing so that you start on the right foot with your new job," said the priest in a nervous manner. Even after cleaning up in the bathroom, she still looked disheveled, and debris from her fall from heaven could still be plainly seen in her white, silken hair.

"Thank you, Father . . .?"

"Thomas, please. You may call me Father Thomas."

"Thank you for your hospitality, but if you don't mind, I need to lie down for some much-needed rest," said the angel in between huge yawns.

"Very well then, I will show you the way . . ."

Quickly, she stood up to follow the priest to her temporary place of residence. Upon arrival, Father Thomas opened the door and led her into where she would be staying, for the time being.

Overall, the look was minimalist at best. Stark, white walls had only one fundamental design—the Almighty God's framed picture hanging above her bed. After her last encounter with the Almighty God, this might not have been the most benign presence that was watching over her. Remembering the horror of God ripping and tearing off her wings, she felt around her shoulder blades with her right hand and felt . . . absolutely nothing. There was no scar or any semblance of what had previously happened, just her human back and nothing more. How depressing . . .

"Are you all right?" asked Father Thomas, noticing that she was inspecting her back.

"Yes, just a small itch that I was scratching, Father," she said, quickly putting her hands down to her sides.

"Very well then, I will leave you to your own devices for tonight, and one of our nuns will be in to give you brand-new clothes for your first day of work. Plain and modest clothes, but they should not be taken for granted . . . it's my gift to you."

Before she could put a word in edgewise, he was already gone without a trace, quietly shutting the door behind himself. Finally alone, she was literally ensconced in complete silence. After all the previous chaos that she had been through, a much-needed rest was definitely in order. So, with her street clothes still on, she climbed into bed and left this forsaken earth on dreams of a whisper . . . until something strange in the middle of the night woke her up.

Startled, Lillith quickly checked her surroundings and saw absolutely nothing. The lights spontaneously turned on by themselves, then turned off all on their own. This happened for several minutes before it suddenly stopped, and she was once again left in the shrouds of darkness to fend for herself.

Chapter Twenty-Three

SOMETHING SINISTER
IS UPON US . . .

Moments later, she felt a cool and squirmy entity slide up her leg and completely rest on top of the center of her stomach. Bravery now taking hold of her, she threw back the bedsheets to reveal a very thin black snake with beady red eyes coiled up on top of her. Next, without hesitation, the black snake coiled up even more as she slowly leaned in to get a better vantage point as to what exactly it was doing . . . Leaping into action, the macabre entity sprang at her face and sunk its fangs deep into the left side of her cheek. Before she could make her next plan of attack against the creature, the black snake mysteriously disappeared out of plain sight, never to be heard from or ever seen again.

Fully awake from the adrenaline, she turned on the lights to try to find the mysterious creature. Where had it come from? How did it receive access to her room? Scanning the room quickly, she soon discovered . . . absolutely nothing at all. Not a trace of the creature could be seen anywhere, which worried her even more.

Taking a quick assessment of her facial injury, she hurried to the mirror. Astonishingly, the left side of her cheek had no identifying marks of any kind, so, confused as ever, she went to bed and dreamed of less benign entities after that whole ordeal.

The next day, a nun lightly knocked on the door outside of Lillith's temporary residence. Waiting a moment, she quietly peeked inside to see if she was still sleeping. Of course, the nun was correct, and she was still sleeping. Bringing in her brand-new clothes for her first day on the job, she felt that something was wrong. Quickly running to the bed, the nun pulled the bed-sheets back to reveal Lillith in a very strange position. Her eyes were bulging out of their sockets, and her face was contorted in some kind of grimace. She appeared to have faced something up close and personal that was extremely sinister upon her final moments on this forsaken earth. Grimacing at the ghastly sight of Lillith's countenance, she felt for a pulse on her neck . . . none was revealed to her. She also put her ear to Lillith's nose to make sure that she was still breathing . . . she was most definitely not.

Panic-stricken, she found Father Thomas in the hall and told him everything that had recently occurred. Thinking logically, he ran into the main study to abruptly call 9-1-1.

"9-1-1, what's your case of emergency?" asked the first responder, with an extreme sense of urgency in her voice.

"This is urgent—I believe we have a deceased woman in our cathedral. I met her yesterday while she was sobbing outside of the cathedral. We all gave her a place to stay, here, for the time being . . . she . . . she . . ." He could not believe what was happening now. In between sobs he stammered, "I . . . I . . . believe that her passing away was far from peaceful." *How could this happen in a house of worship?* he quietly thought to himself.

"What was the cause of death, sir, if I may ask?" asked the first responder, with legitimate concern in her voice.

"Unknown," said Father Thomas, quickly gathering his emotions to remain calm and collected for everyone during this abrupt crisis.

"All right, sir, we will have two responders on the way as soon as possible."

"Thank you."

"You're welcome, sir." The responder abruptly hung up before he could even utter another word.

Several minutes later, two men in an ambulance showed up and began knocking on the gigantic cathedral entrance. Quickly, the priest ushered them in and led the way toward the now deceased woman. *In our cathedral . . . an innocent woman died.* He could not rip free of the horrific image that was still captured on her face—a look of sheer terror, just before her innocent life was cruelly taken away. Once inside, the men set to work on finalizing a cause of death for the individual. Approximately twenty minutes later, they confirmed without a reasonable doubt that Lillith was now dead. After a thorough investigation, they concluded that the actual cause of death for the individual was a catastrophic heart attack . . . something of this magnitude . . . had scared her to death.

What entity could have caused such a scare? In her last moments on this forsaken earth, what had caused the sheer terror so plainly *still* written on her face? Many questions to ponder, and yet, still many more that would haunt his dreams . . . unanswered questions about her untimely death that would remain a mystery for all eternity.

After the men left with the body, to later have the coroner pick it up, no one could remain in that room. There was too much sadness that resided there, and whatever had frightened her to death, its macabre presence still felt like it lingered in the room . . . strange.

A complete silence passed between the nun and the priest—some silent, empty void to possibly fill up all of the ill feelings they both had about this most unfortunate incident. Later on, their overall thoughts and ideas were to bless the room with holy water, just in case the presence was not something that should be allowed in the cathedral, just as a cautionary procedure to conduct at a later time. Well, soon, rather than later, as far as they were both concerned.

Cautionary procedures needed to be enacted soon, as something strange stirred within the mirror of that ill-suited room where Lillith had died. As if trapped within the mirror, an entity of darkness stirred inside, almost knocking it to the floor. Mere moments later, a smoky, gray image could be seen with eyes that could pierce into the depths of your very soul, even if she was an overall soulless creature herself.

Those eyes belonged to me . . . Desdemona . . . and my little snake routine actually happened. Yet, I played a defective trick with the mirror that made it seem that Lillith was fine, when she was actually starting her overall turn for the worse. Worse . . . wasn't she the one who ended up killing *me*? An angel falls to earth for a reason. I noticed that happening . . . I was far off in the distance in the forest and witnessed it. Well, my overall spirit did, and now that I was well studied in the afterlife, there was no telling what I could do to people now . . . my powers were now unlimited.

Creeping out of the mirror, I quickly retracted when I heard the priest and the nun enter the room together. A ceremony with holy water was about to commence, and I absolutely wanted nothing to do with it. *Oh, what perfect timing,* I silently thought to myself. As the two began to cross my path in front of the mirror that I was currently trapped in, I swiftly made my move. Springing into action, my arms flung out of the mirror and grabbed the priest and the nun by the back of their heads. Their eyes bulging in complete shock, they had no idea as to what would occur next . . . the day they both left this forsaken earth. Gripping tighter, I yanked them both into the mirror and let them live with me for the time being . . . in the ninth circle in hell.

All mirrors were just the gateway for any of us to get to you . . . sad but true.

Tragedy.